LaToya Shahira Williams

Chicken Change

Change

Reloaded

Written by: LaToya Shahira Williams

This is the Sequel

To

LaToya Shahira Williams

Chicken Change: The Code of the Streets Tied up in a Love Affair....
The Novel that had readers asking and wondering...

"Who did it?"

Acknowledgements

What an incredible feeling it is to be able to share with the world The Visions in my Head. I am so humble to present part two of my first published novel Chicken Change; since the beginning of it all, I have had an amazing support team and without them, I could not have gotten this book finished.

Firstly, I have to thank God for listening to my prayer and giving me strength to overcome my uncertainties, which stopped me at one point in time from following my dreams. To my beautiful daughter Alayah, this is for you and this is for us. Special thanks to my family and friends. My sisters for supporting me, my Mother and Nana for praying for me. This is for all of you, including my Aunts and Uncles, cousins too; naming you all will be too much to do. Those that matter know just who you are! Therefore, I am screaming in print I love my family, friends, and all of my supporters, I am thankful to have people like you in my life. May God bless each of you! I hope you enjoy reading Chicken Change: Reloaded...

With love,

LaToya Shahira Williams

Chicken Change: Reloaded

Written by: LaToya Shahira Williams

IS THE ORIGINAL WORK

OF

The Eye of the Gun...

A King that crowns a Bad Bitch for his Queen...

Be wary... Not every Bad Bitch is a Queen...

Bad Bitches break men... A real Bad Bitch will build
her King...

-LaToya Shahira Williams

Prologue

Unfinished Business

I had a strong feeling prior to going to New York to meet up with Kathy, and give her my side of the story, on how I exposed the El Pablo Gang and the Jameson brothers. One of which I found out was my biological father. Who would have thought after four long years, my past was going to fuck with my present. When I left that life, alone I buried that broken bitch Deandra Harper, hoping I never had to let her back into my skin. I finally had closure, something I always wanted and felt like I deserved.

I did not ask for the streets to kidnap me and sell me off to an obsessed dick thirsty whore. Who was jealous of my mother! My mother a bitch who so-called loved me to death; stood in my face and never acknowledged herself to me... I would have never guessed that cat-eye staring, evil looking tramp Keliney was the person I cried for at night. The one I prayed for, the one who birth me, and once upon a time took care of me... that snob was my mother. I was done, and I wanted nothing more with that life.

I thought I had broken all ties with Greg, I didn't even question him on why he never told me I was breaking bread with my mother, who he knew and knew I wanted more than anything in life. I gave that pussy a break and I saved his ass from spending life in prison. Although he protected me from finding out the truth about both him and my mother, I forgave him. I never told on him and I never turned my back on him. I was still that ride or die bitch for him.

My King Thomas had my back since the day I met him; I could not have asked for a more loving and understanding man to marry me and father my only child. During the prosecutions of the fools I helped to put behind bars, Thomas and I wedded in secrecy. We had a private wedding on the Big Island, Hawaii; it was just the two of us and that is all that mattered to us. I did not even tell Taylor I was getting married, I did not want anything to mess up our big day. I was enjoying my life as a wife and a mother. Journey has taught me so much about myself I did not know. My three-year-old inspired me to be the mother I never had. I guarded her in the same ways a lion does her cubs. With Thomas, I was able to give our baby girl a life neither one of us had. Yeah

Thomas had his family but he never had that bond like him and I shared with our daughter.

When I got that phone call, and that person on the other end of the phone told me they had sideswiped my family off the road; somewhere between Pennsylvania and New Jersey, I snapped. We had traveled to the states on different flights, Thomas would not let me come alone; we was going to meet up after my interview. Kathy was pleading with me to call the authorities, but the mother in me could not do it and the thug in me was not having it.

I knew I had only a few hours, if that to find my family alive. I had a six-sense about the whole shit. I never left home without my guns either. I always kept one in my purse, one in my baby bag, one in my waist and one around my ankle. My bodyguards had permission to check a few guns into their luggage, so we flew into the state legal. Even though I had burned the shit that used to hurt, in the back of my mind I still lived in fear. I knew that one day I was going to meet up with all the shit I had burned. So I made sure I was ready for anything, and I was not going out without putting up a fight.

My bodyguards were the truth, three big buff dudes down for anything. Two of which served in the army and the other one was a trained assassin we found on the streets of Mahe' Island, where we lived in Africa. My family and I were planning to return to living in the states after I did my interview with Kathy. I was ready to walk the streets as me. We found a nice quiet place out in the sticks of South Carolina. My world crumbled when I heard what sounded like Greg's voice on the phone.

Since running to the police was not an option for me at the time, my bodyguard's snatched Kathy, the reporter and her camera operator and took them with us. They handcuffed them, after we put them in our truck, which we had parked in the back of the news studio. I apologized to her and told her I was going to give her the story of her career. If she was not the top reporter in the nation by now! I was going to make her the top! I told her, for her safety she needed to stay with me.

I was lying but I was going to do my best to keep us all alive. However, my family was first. My bodyguard was the bomb! Martin was skilled in electronics; I got him to tap into Greg's security cameras, before I went straight into that house and tore shit up. It took Martin twenty-minutes to show me just where that nigga was. We sat two blocks away from the house him and I had in Alpine, New Jersey. That trifling ass bitch had the nerve to move another bitch into the house. Complete proof his ass was not shit.

I just wanted my husband and child back, so I did what any mother would have done if she knew who the culprit was... I remembered the floor plan of the house, so I knew the security system was on a separate emergency line. Therefore, we were able to cut the electricity to his house, while I kept one eye on him at all times.

My timing was perfect, even though I moved on to the rich lands with my billionaire, husband and daughter, I kept my association with the thugs. My bodyguard Terrance picked the lock on the back door; we got in without making a sound. Slowly with our guns drawn and loaded... I eased the doorknob on the master suite. Moreover, I cocked my glock back... and I pointed it to the back of Greg's head. I could have had my boys to do it but this one was personal! He was deep in that pussy... from the looks of it he was fucking that hoe good...she was bitching, going crazy on her back. As the lasers of my bodyguards, riffles pointed to both Greg's and his bitch heads... I demanded the return of my family the way the streets taught me! I shot him no questions asked. The heat of my bullet surfed through the back of Greg's thigh.

"Hello... how are you doing? Shoot first ask questions later right. Yeah I was taught by the best right? Well I got your message, what's up? Why are you fucking with me? I mean my daughter... I can see why you picked to hate on

5

my man... oops my fucking husband. But my baby, I thought we were better than that... turn around so you can see my face..." I said standing over top of his and hers naked bodies. I was hoping it was Alison I was dying to meet her. While turning around Greg was hissing and grunting, I could not feel his pain but I knew he was in pain.

"Bitch you shot me... you fucking shot me..." was all he could say for the moment. While his chick laid there screaming, that trick was going bananas. Tim took a pillow and smashed it onto her mouth, within seconds Greg and the girl was duct-taped to the headboard of the bed.

"Who are you sweetheart?" I asked her...

"Bridget..." She yelled back, and then I taped her mouth closed.

"Bridget honey I am going to need for you to calm down. I do not want you; just consider yourself in the right place but at the wrong time. Do not be scared I just want to talk to Greg. I had to shoot him, that is the only way I can talk to him... he understands... it's the code of the streets... so be a doll and be quiet or I will shoot you too... just because." I said, and I was calm... I guess that was the scariest thing about my approach.

"Surprised you hun Mr. Weston? I guess looking into my eyes you are saying I look like my fucking dad, yet I act so much like my fucking mother hun?"

"Fuck you bitch what did I do to you?" Greg replied...

"Look pussy stop playing stupid... give me my family back and I won't kill you. I want both my husband and my daughter back alive." A part of me wanted to cry but I held it in.

"Dee I don't know what you are talking about I don't have your family..." Greg cried out.

"Look we can do this two ways, give me back my family and I won't shoot you again! On the other hand, do not give me my family and I will shoot you in the arms, chest, and legs; flip you over and shoot you in the back, cut your dick off and make you chew it up and swallow it before I put nine bullets in your brain. Then post pictures of your guts all over the internet. Don't fuck with me... give me back my family." I blacked out in words...

"What are you talking about? I do not have your family... you know me... what makes you think I stole your African booty scratcher... and baby... Dee I am over you... you crazy bitch..." Greg shouted.

"Oh you got jokes, why do you want to play stupid with this bitch that is strapped to take lives to get mines." Then in front of everybody, I took a seat on the bed beside Greg and I started to caress his penis with my hand. I plucked it then I started to rub it. Then just as I thought that pussy got hard.

"Get the fuck off me...," he yelled...

"Ha-ha just like I thought... I still get you hard like a pickle..."

"Fuck you... I should pee on you..."

"I fucking dare you... do it and watch me cut it off..." Mona tormented me growing up so I mocked her in my own way. Then before I could say another word, my phone ringed...

"What goes around comes back around... The Code Of The Streets Is Broken..."

Chapter 1

The Street Code

"**H**ello..." I answered the phone...

"You are a not as smart as I first had in mind..." the voice replied through the other end of the phone.

"Who is this, and what do you want?" I questioned, as I stood up and walked over to the window to glance out of the drapes...

"You ran straight to the fire, just like I thought you would not; but your stupid ass did... I was giving you the benefit of doubt...tell me... did I say I was Greg when I called you a few hours ago to tell you I had your family?"

"What... Who is this and how do you know me?"

"I am your worst nightmare Bitch and I want my fucking money..."

"You must have me confused with somebody else I do not owe any one anything and who said I am the person you are looking for..."

"Bitch I am looking at you right now sleeve jerking that bum ass pussy that robbed me. I am not a cold killer, I like to sit and watch my enemies die by the hands of their own people... now let us talk business... I always ask questions before I shoot. I know the Uptown players do it the opposite way, I know for a fact Melly stashed my money in your name, and I know Gee helped her. However, what they forgot to do was kill me. Rule number one in this game you always body bag the bodies up yourself." As he talked I signaled for my bodyguards to take aim at the window and at the bedroom door. I covered the camera in Greg's room and then as I untied him and his Bitch... shots ringed out... Boom...Boom...boom...boom....boom...boo...ba, ba, ba, boom....

I could not believe it my bodyguard Martin went flying into the air... the kidnapper was in the house. I had no idea as to who it was... I was bout it...but I was not ready for this twist of gunfire. I was strapped and ready to gunfight with Greg... but certainly not ready for the unidentified person. As fast as we could dodge the flying bullets, we ran into the closet.

Greg and I both knew about the hidden pass way, which we put in place when he and I moved in. The tunnel was for just in case something like this was to happen, beings though Greg was heavy in the streets. Inside the tunnel were back steps that led to a bunker underground. Once inside of the bunker we could get out through the sewer that was in the woods not far from the New Jersey Turnpike.

The bunker was loaded with clean clothes, gas masks, nonperishable foods, and most importantly ammunition and explosives. From the inside of the closet nobody could tell it had a secrete entrance; once the floor door was pulled tight, the carpet matched without a trace. One by one, we entered the bunker, I completely forgot about Kathy and her camera operator we left behind in the car. Greg entered first then Bridget and I at the same time, last to enter were my bodyguards Terrence and Tim.

"Dee I told you I didn't have anything to do with your baby being kidnaped... you know me Dee... and bitch you shot me damn, we got to get out of here, my leg is bleeding crazy I know it trailed..." Greg said grunting while putting on his clothes that was stored in the tunnel and passing Bridget something to put on.

"Look nigga I had no choice, you always told me to shoot first and ask questions later, so I thought you was the person I was after, I found you and I shot you. Now I want to know who is after us..." I replied as I tried to get my thoughts together.

"I don't know, the only person money Melly and I took was the money from the distribution house that belonged to Carlos."

"But it can't be Carlos he is in jail, so who else is out there you forgot about?" I was scared like shit...

"I don't know..." Greg replied

"Shush, somebody is coming how do we get out of here?" Tim whispered...

"Oh shit I told you I trailed blood... damn it... tie my leg up and let's go... Greg replied as he passed me an ace-bandage and some antiseptic ointment. Quickly I poured the ointment onto his thigh and wrapped his womb.

"Look what is done, is done... now get us out of this shit, I am sorry..." I was beyond frightened...

"I knew I should have stayed home this is some bullshit..." Bridget cried out...

"Shut up bitch this is the odds of fucking with a street nigga, if you ain't about this life you better get it together or you are going to die first...."I said trying to chump Bridget...

"We don't have time to argue..." Terrance said as he put his fingers up to his mouth to quiet us. On the other side of the door were four other doors so unless there was an army outside the bunkers door it was going to take the shooter a second to find us.

Quickly grabbing all that we could carry, we hauled ass out of the bunker, and headed to the pass way, with deep hope to reach the sewer. I could have gagged when the strong human poop smell entered my nose, I could taste the smell in my mouth. The only thing on my mind was getting out alive.   I was not worried about Martin lifeless body, which was still in the main house. I was not even thinking about my missing family for the fact my life was in jeopardy.

Chapter 2

Kathy's High

"Kathy... what the fuck was that, we have to get out of here!"

"I don't know but, I think we just witnessed a major crime or some shit...I have to call Christa..." I replied to my cameraman Bill...

"Fuck her Kathy they kidnapped us... I didn't sign up for this shit give me the fucking phone I am calling the police..." Bill responded in a frantic tone of voice.

"Look this is the job you signed up for, so stop acting like a fucking cock sucker..." I then yelled back...

"Kathy what are you trying to do? We need to get out of here... I am telling you something is not right, and I do not want to be caught up in a conspiracy to a fucking crime... job or no fucking job, fuck this fucking job bitch!" I do not think I have ever seen Bill so paranoid before; and we had been working together for years. The two of us had been to some of the toughest countries reporting.

"Bill calling me a bitch is not going to hurt my feelings, I live for this type of raw energy! This could be our big break. Now reach into my bra and get my phone out... after that crap Christa pulled with sending me to Australia and not showing up... I caught on to her game... now I want my freaking story ..."

"Kathy!" Bill called out...

"Just do it, I am going to turn around and you are going to reach under my right breast and get my phone... don't get fresh I know your wife. I would hate to blackmail you in front of her..." I replied laughing aloud... trying to persuade him to get on board with me.

"Fuck you Kathy, you are a slut and everybody knows it, you cross me and I will leak those photos I have of you giving brain on the main vein in the boardroom... fuck with me and I will end your fucking cum to the top career! My wife is not to be played with!"

"Just do it...and for the record... I will suck and fuck the Presidents cock, record it and blackmail him for the White House press secretary seat... judge your paycheck... I work hard for my name... Northwestern University graduate!"

"Kathy duck..." Bill grabbed me as the two of us slid down between the back row seats of the truck... five masked gunmen came running down the street, of what was supposed to be an upscale luxurious community. Alpine, New Jersey was not notorious for this type of activity. The men stormed passed the SUV and hopped into what looked like a getaway car. What a good look it was...

"Hurry up, Billy grab the phone I got the car license plate number"... and with my tongue, I typed the plate number into my mobile phone...

"Damn we have to get out of here... Who was that?" Bill questioned.

"I don't know but it was not the group that brought us here..." I replied in a rather calming tone of voice. My adrenaline was running on a high, I cannot explain the feeling; this had never happened to me... I knew this story oh too well and I knew it was a history bookmarker. Melody was a good friend of mine; we had become close when I met her at the New York's, Mayors Ball for his inauguration.

"All man we got to get out of here like right now, right fucking now shit..." Bill's bitching was turning me on, for some odd reason. Bill was not attractive, a little scruffy, a little buddy kind of type guy.

"Stop bitching Billy, this could be our big break, I could get that head correspondent position..." I could not help but to reply simmering in laughter. Oh, he was too cute, something like a lost puppy.

"You are insane I am calling the police, yeah the fucking police! I got a wife and two kids at home, not to mention my fucking dog bitch I quit..."

"Billy! Are you serious? What do you need? Do you need your cock sucked until the gun smoke blow? You know I could ease your tension?" My unethical work ethics was not working in my favor, this go round, I thought to myself.

"I am good you probably got something you can't get rid of..." Bill replied... Not hurting my feeling and not helping me to snap back into career mode either. Therefore, after we untied ourselves, I bent over and groped Bill's penis anyway... knowingly committing a sexual harassment case. I was overly hungry to add this story on my resume.

"Get off me I am married..."

"But I got you hard...Billy" I teased hoping he would take the joke and lighten up a bit...

"Fuck you move so I can hotwire this car... nasty just unprofessional. I am a hunter I like to chase; an easy catch is a STD trying to spread. Now I am in charge of this show, call Christa and see if you can get in contact with her if she is alive anyway... I going to use this phone right here and I am going to call the police... and stop calling me Billy... Kathleen... Oh shit somebody beat me to it...lets go..." so as the gated community was starting to fill up with police, Bill backed up and drove out of the back way and on to the main road.

"Who is this?" a female voice answered...

"Christa is that you?" I asked...

"Kathy where are you?"

"Bill it's her she is alive... Looking for you, I want my story..."

"You are such a white girl..." Christa replied...

"So they tell me... where are you?"

"Meet me on the turnpike fourteen miles from the Lincoln Tunnel Heliport... when you get to the seventh marker pull over and watch your back..." then Christa hung up the phone...

Part 2

Back in the Woods with Dee

"Dee how do you know you can trust her..." Terrance asked...

"Because I know, and she knows I will shoot her if I had too..." I replied...

"So you are a killer now Dee I never known you to be a body bagger?" Greg added...

"Yeah just like you thought you knew all of my capabilities... for my daughter I have no limit. Kathy is a rider I did my homework on her, like me... she has no limit. Now that cameraman I don't know about him, so when they get here Terrance and Greg y'all tag-team him... and as for you Bridget, if you want to stay alive you better stay chill...Tim watch her..." For twenty extra minutes Terrance, Tim, Greg, Bridget and I waited in the woods that lined the highway's lanes. I could not believe we managed to get away from that gunman. I had never been more terrified then what I was before this point.

My heart was racing I could have had a heart attack that night. Kathy and Bill pulled up just in time… "Hurry up get in y'all…" Bill called out. Just in time, because we started hearing footsteps creep through the woods from afar. Whomever that was shooting, followed us through the bunkers tunnel. We quickly jumped into the back seat, as Bill sped off.

"Do not go back to New York… we have to crisscross our steps." Greg answered back.

"I got this now… what the fuck is going on?" Bill said, showing some authority.

"Look I don't know, this is Greg and his Bridget… when we got into the house I caught these two gripping the sheets, I shot him, then as I was going in grilling him, my phone ringed and then someone shot through the door they killed Martin. He didn't even have a chance." I said trying to get the story out and catch my breath at the same time.

"Look I was able to get a look at the shooters, it was five men in ski masks, this is the plate number they got away in…I got a person, that can tell me if the car was stolen or not. He can link it back to the owner." Kathy added…

"Look we don't need nobody extra in this until we find out who we are up against." Tim said who was also trying to catch his breath…

"Well it's a starting point… I want you to find your daughter and husband like right now right now… But you are going to have to start checking possible screwballs off the list." Bill commented.

"You're right we got to figure this shit out and narrow it down. It's not going to be too long before the FED's are going to start looking for us..." Greg said adding his two sense in again... As everyone was conversing, I zoned out... I did not want to fall any deeper into masterminding another bad decision. I was holding back tissues full of tears; all I wanted was my daughter back and Thomas. While Kathy was chasing her career's high, I was slowly dying in the inside. How could my selfish ways allow the only two and one half people I loved slip from my arms?

I was praying hard to find my baby alive. I was praying her daddy was keeping her safe. The more I tried to pray for the best, reality was setting in; whomever that was shooting at us, was nothing to play with. It was going to take more than a prayer to save my family. I was lost for words, ideas, and frightened out of my mind. I just sat back and watched that valley girl chase her dream of being the next Barba Walters. Kathy eyes were beaming red: if this had been a scene in a movie, she was going to get an Oscar, an Emmy and a Golden Globe. It was because of me Martin was dead, and it was because of me we was in this shit. I was starting to lose my gangster. The sun was starting to rise by the time we had reached Ohio.

"We have to change cars, and drive back south. Keeping our tracks clean is the best thing we can do right now. Y'all two need to get back to work, as if nothing happened. We are going to need access to the latest news. Besides, y'all cannot go missing, because a smart detective is

going to link you with us. We will keep in touch."
Then just like a Gee Greg was calling all the shots,
or so he thought.

"Not a good idea, we were supposed to fly out
on assignment at 11:00am... so if we are going to
act normal we have to go to our location... we will
stop by the rental car dealer and pick up our car
and take things from there..." Bill said cutting
Greg off...

"And where is that?" Tim asked...

"Mt Holly Penitentiary, not far from here..."
Kathy stated...

"Wait...stop...stop the car....Melly is at Mt.
Holly..." I screamed aloud ...

"Yeah I know you and I are going to pay Miss.
Valery a visit. It was not my intension to bring you
with me but since you promised me my career
high story... you are coming..." Kathy switched up
the game on me... she forced to pay my mother a
visit in jail.... While Bill took over the only loaded
pistol, he took control over Greg, Tim, Terrance
and Bridget as they sat in the car. While, Kathy
and I went in to visit Melly.... A moment I was not
wishing for... I just wanted to forget her, my anger
towards her, made me hate her. Yeah I hated that
I wanted to love my mother again...

Chapter 3

Meeting Mommy

After washing my hands several times in the restroom to remove the gun powder residue, that could have been on my hands; I waited with both daunting and pass-aggression emotions running through my head, until I was called back to get scanned by security. I was hoping my nerves would get me turned around and set home; I was praying the hand scanner would pick up the gunpowder residue.

However, with the luck I was having I gotten passed security, without any issues. As soon as those doors slammed behind me, I crumbled. All of a sudden, I started to get cold; I could feel a draft blowing down my back. I never had the chance to talk to Keliney after I found out who she really was; I never wrote to her, I never tried to contact her. It was like meeting a total stranger you had stereotyped and hated. I do not think I would have felt like this towards her if she had come clean about herself to me on her own. I would not have told a sole about her, she would have been my best-kept secret. Nevertheless, she did not trust me enough to confide into me, therefore I placed her into my fuck you file, and I hated her.

Thicker then what I last remember her being, I finally was able to see her long pretty hair again, which was braided into cornrows. Damn her hair was long the plats ended close to her waist. She was pretty, gazing at her from afar; I could not imagine her, having to have lived that hard-knocked life she had. Standing about five feet six inches, about one hundred and fifty something pounds... stood the body that gave birth to me.

I could had slaughtered Taylor for telling the cops Keliney was Melly; when I found out I didn't say anything to the cops, I only told Taylor. The biggest mistake ever, I only wanted the Jameson's brothers to go down for kidnapping Shaun and me. I was tired of living in pain. Kathy nudged me to walk over with her to meet Melly. Quickly I got it together, thinking Kathy just said I had to go, but she did not say I had to talk...

"Hello, Miss Valery, I am Kathy Armstrong, thank you so much for choosing me to tell your side of the story. I brought with me your daughter Christa, just like you asked..." and before Melly could say a word I jumped right in...

"Bitch you set me up Kathy; you planned this whole thing didn't you?" I broke my cool quick...

"Name calling is not going to get you anywhere sweetheart... now sit down you owe me..." Kathy replied...

"I don't have time to play your little games, do you have my family bitch..." I commented back...

"Hello Chrissy..." Melly spoke to me... Melly spoke to me...I did not know what to think... when Melly spoke to me... I just kept repeating to myself... Melly spoke to me... until I blurted out...

"You don't know me to call me that... Melody..."

"I can understand that, but let me just say this for the record... I am sorry, and what I did, I did it for you. I never meant to hurt you, or to cause you any pain. I know you are too hurt to understand or to accept my sincere apology but its okay I don't expect you too." I could not believe Melly was talking to me as herself and not as I knew her.

"That is not what I came here for... which one of your enemies is after me and kidnapped my daughter and my fucking husband... I am over our happy ending... I just want my real family back..."

"What... how do I know? I been in this jail for four years or so and I got another couple of decades to go...But I am not the one mad at you. It wasn't too long before all of my shit was going to catch up with me..." her nonchalant demeanor was irking me to the max. "The person who has my family told me, you have everything to do with the bullets that grazed passed my head last night and the reason why my child and husband are missing." while the two of us argued back and forth Kath decided to jump in...

"Melody what happened the night Christa was taken from your home?" Kathy asked as she took notes with the pieces of paper and pencil she had gotten from the guard.

"Well it was about eight o'clock in the morning when I got word Carlos had his boys to raid my house and take my daughter. I kept Christa up like royalty. I was kingpin and my daughter was the princess. Gucci and the finest linens only touched my baby's body..."

"Do you know why he took your daughter?"

"No... I did not do anything to him... I never stole from him, I never told on him... yeah I may had slept his brother but Carlos was never my man. I had spontaneous sexual encounters with my boss and we had a love child together, who the streets kidnapped from the hospital... I never had the chance to meet King Carlos... that is what I named him. I was young and stupid. Vanessa was always Carlos wife... she had his heart not me. I just had his drugs and business..." as Melly spoke I sat unresponsive; trying match the puzzled pieces.

"Why can't you answer the question? What happened the day Christa was taken?" Kathy rejoined, as I sat there waiting for her to answer the questions, I was nervous to ask her...

"Kathy you keep cutting me off... damn can I talk?" Melody changed her tone of voice and facial expression... looking and sounding like she wanted to say... Bitch... or more so like she had been talking to a friend. Kathy and Melly's behavior was starting to look as if they had known each other before; yet playing a role of some sort that had been pre-rehearsed.

"Yes please talk..." Kathy said returning the floor to Melly.

"Okay...Okay so like I was saying the day I lost Christa I didn't know what was going on. Word on the streets was saying I jacked up some drop on the docks, but that could not have been true, I never made drops on the docks. I never did business with the Chester Choppers. I didn't know Antonio was a part of the Choppers either. He was always the nerdy type who wanted to be down but was not build for the life Carlos and I lived.

He raped me repeatedly one day, when I was in the distribution house alone... when I saw it was him I opened the door thinking everything was good. When he realized I was in there by myself, he started talking about how I let him down; but I could not understand what he was talking about I was too busy trying not to lose count of the money I had just counted.

The pushers had just brought in their profits from the night runs and I was putting together inventory for the mid-day crew and rubber-banding bills by the thousands... whatever Antonio was babbling about I was not trying to hear. So I guess when he noticed my ignorance he punched me in my stomach. He kicked to the floor; he dragged me into the back office when he heard the noontime pushers coming in.

I was the only one who had the keys and passcodes to the back office, and he knew it. He stripped me naked, and forced his self on to me... he raped me repeatedly for hours, my mouth was duct-taped closed and my hands was placed behind my back tied with tape. I was in love with Carlos, even though he was not mine. When he let me go, I rushed passed Jeff and a few other crewmembers, I was sick...but I could not kill him because of my loyalty to Carlos. Because of the code of the streets, I did not tell on him; however, I planned to get revenge on him.

When I found out I was pregnant with Christa I told Carlos it was his baby...I did everything I could to protect her after she was born. I was working triple time to grind up money to take her out of the misery in which I lived... I purchased a house in Alpine, New Jersey... I stashed a few millions for us to live off of... but my plans got twisted when I found out Carlos was responsible for killing my aunt who had raised me and who took care of Christa when I was working... he not only killed her but he took my daughter... for no reason. He broke the code of the streets.

Someone had shot up my house about three times before then and I did not know why... Nobody knew where I lived, except my brother Jeff. I did not live in the hood like the other workers... hence I did not know what was going on.... If I had known Carlos and I had beef I would have took him out a long time ago. I was a sharp shooter..."

"You say you were a sharp shooter, but your loyalty caused you not to tell on Antonio or kill him for raping you... you knew Carlos was behind your children disappearing...and you also knew he murdered your aunt... I don't get it... what is it you are hiding or biting your lip to say...." Kathy took the words right out of my mouth... I was still flabbergasted...

"Look I really don't know what happened and I don't want to talk about it anymore..." Melody was starting to shut down... this bitch was bipolar I thought. Her ugliness was starting to show.

"Okay I can respect that and truth be told I don't want to know.... All I want to know is who money you stashed in my name..." I hopped in and questioned...

"What are you talking about? I gave Gee all the money I had, so he could take care of you darling..."

"Gee had the millions you put up for us?"

"Yeah...something like that...." she said chuckling...

"Something like what lady? And what the hell is so funny?" oh I was heated.

"I had old money, new money.... chicken change money and fish money... rich money and bitch money... all my money was my money. I do not know what you are talking about honey bunny! The weight I pushed after Gee and I took control was all my money... those bricks I had you saw that day, were counted ... I don't owe nobody... I am my own boss bitch. Pow..." Then as she stopped clapping her hands, rap singing her childish rhyme, she took silence and the room went quiet, for approximately two minutes as we sat looking at one another... then I snapped...

"What the fuck... you're a rapper now... you know what... fuck you I am over this... you couldn't even save me when I was little, and your bird caged ass can't help me now I see either! You never gave a fuck about me and you know it. You are a criminal just like the fucking players you balled with... I just told you my daughter, was abducted, as well as my fucking husband, because of someone who is after you. You know what... I don't need you; I never did, even when I thought I did...

You are not my mother, never was and never will be. Fuck you, hope you rot in hell and receive more than half of the bullshit I had to deal with over the years. You never gave a fuck about me, shit when I met you and did not have a clue as to who you really was; never did you identify yourself to me. You let Greg corrupt me and break my fucking heart. You knew what kind of slime ball he was, you knew about all the shit he was into, and what type of life he lived. Yet your bitch ass never once took my back or stood up for me. Greg slapped me in your face and you sat in that jail and watched, as if we were girlfriends' double dating jailbirds! Robin Hood, hell you hardly said five fucking words to me in one meeting time... too damn busy worrying about your fucking self and your stolen funds.

Mucky bitch you set me up from day one... day fucking one and for that, I hate you. The difference between you and me is.... I gave birth and on that day I chosen to be a mother I chosen to be the best fucking mother I could be. I changed my fucking life for the better not the worst... you on the other hand never gave a fuck about me or my brother.... You should have just aborted us or shot us your damn self, because I rather be dead then to have this fucking hurt felt feeling, which you have beaten on me.

Fuck, you to the highest number in math... one hundred nonillion, billion, million, nine-hundred, ninety-nine thousand power... fuck you to the highest power. You will reap what you sow. Boom how you like them apples... and Fuck you too Kathy kiss my ass!" Then I got up after my Oscar Award winning performance and stormed to the exit.

I was over being cordial I could not take it any longer. I was feeling like fuck crazy Kathy and her story. The only reason why I said yes to do an interview with her; was because she was the only reporter who offered to pay me my asking price... I never knew I sold myself to the devil, or this would be how I had to pay her back. I didn't care anymore; I was feeling like shoot me bitch... fucking shoot me, in the back of my fucking head and kick that shit. I was over feeling as if I was stuck in a fucking circle! I had hours to find out where my family was, or if they were still breathing. I was ready to give up chasing. My mind was cruising out of control I was angry and on top of angry I was hurt.

I walked right passed the truck where Greg, Bill and the rest of the gang was waiting. I pretended not to hear Bill call me, as I ranted straight up the hill to walk into the oncoming traffic that was driving on the high way. I was not contemplating suicide but I was looking for my get away. When Bill came running behind me I blacked out and body slammed him to ground. I had become a black belt in karate, instead of joining a gym I took up kick boxing, karate and boxing.

The only one that was able to stop me was Greg. Tim, Terrance or Bridget didn't even bother to try me after they seen how mad I was and all the pain Bill was in. I probably could have picked up a car the way I was feeling, maybe not a car but a person four times my size.

"Yo Dee stop come here Dee... what happened what is wrong... what did she say Dee? Talk to me..." Greg shouted while slow jogging and limping behind me. I turned around and took a seat on the guardrail, on the side of the highway. His belligerent tone of voice was all I needed to stop; I still loved him.

"What's not wrong...?" I cried out...

"I am going to do my best to help you baby girl, but you can't give up now, I am going to make sure you get to see your baby girls pretty smile again. She looks just like you Dee, and pretty just like you... I kind of feel like all this shit is my fault. I should have protected you better. I fucked up..." Then the tears stopped...as Greg babbled on... I had one more person to tell off from the heart...

Chapter 4

While I am Living

"**I** can't say that I've missed you, and I can't say that I don't… but I've been sort of happy living in Africa with my husband and my daughter. I never wanted to be happier in my life as Thomas and Journey has made me feel. I finally got that feeling I was always looking for. I never knew that feeling could not be found, it had be built; but I can't say that I have completeness, a part of me honestly wonder what it could have been with us…

I have to get this off my chest and I have to say what I should have said back then. Holding on to this baggage is killing me; I am so over this fucking feeling. I could sit here and cry to you about Cupid shooting me with his arrow, I can tell you that my match was standing right under my eyes. I can tell you it was love at first sight. I could brag about how we do not fuss or fight. All of that might be true. However, if I do not make it out of this alive I am going to tell you just how I feel.

I was not over us, when I fell in love with Thomas, a part of me still wanted you. I am not going to lie you meant the world to me; I did not call you my King for nothing. Greg you were everything. You crushed my dreams, my future and my spirit; when you put the blockers on me and you threw me out of the picture, like a cheap pair of shoes. I had nothing.

You sold me a future and then you took it from me. I don't even know how I got in the middle of yours and Melly's bullshit! That Bitch looked me in my eyes today for the first time... it was one of the bloodcurdling visions ever. I am terrified; I don't know what to do. I could have sworn that was you on the other end of the phone. Telling me you took my family. Who is after us and want me dead next to you? Who is it damn it?" Immediately I broke down into tears, on the side of the road with Greg... for the first time in years I was feeling like I did when I first met him... I could not get my curse words out.

"I know Dee and I am sorry, I am happy for you, so if I don't make it out alive... I want you to know... I never wanted to hurt you! I never wanted to make you cry; and I never wanted to make you unhappy! All I ever wanted to do was make you smile. Yeah I went about things the wrong way, but I was a self-centered boy then. I was not a man. I didn't even care about life. All I knew was money, drugs and pussy. Truth, you was never just pussy to me.

A female's intuition always see what the eyes try to hide... However, it takes a real woman to see it, and know her worth. She knows her worth is more valuable than putting up with a boy's lies and deceit. Head held high she could walk away and laugh at the trash she left behind. The truth never hurts her, it only teaches her not to settle for less. Therefore, with that, I can respect your decision to leave me in the past.

Baby girl you are not missing nothing when it concerns me. I will never be the man you need to complete you. All I can do for you is to put you on your back and skeet all in you. I have my flaws ... I don't deserve you and I never did. I am a gangster and I live a gangster life. I am not husband material, I give rings but I do not mean nothing more or less than that... A man like me don't deserve a woman like you. I am a street runner Dee."

"Greg I am not saying I want you back I know what type of person you are! All I want is your help; all I need is your help... Please just help me find my baby! Get out of your feelings! so while I am still alive I want you to know that I aborted the baby I told you I lost..." then as fast as I could, I got up and started to walk off, before he could slap me... if he felt the need too or whatever... so when he grabbed me I went into defense mode... "So while I am living... I need you to know why I said fuck you... I had an epiphany... and in that moment when I suddenly woke up, and realized, I was in the wrong type of relationship.

In that moment, my mind started to wonder and in that second, I started to think about what if and the maybes. That is when I finally visualize the picture. Of what true happiness means to me, mentally I gained that since of completeness... The vision of us suddenly faded away from my heart and my mind. It was that feeling when your greed sets in, and your emotions takes a hold over you.

Your anger is the first to fight its way out, your strength is second to fall. Your pride will not let you stay instead your emotions fills your face full of tears and thoughts. That is when you get up and handle your shit like a fucking woman and not just any fucking woman but the woman you were born to be. With the steam blowing out of your ears and the adrenaline rushing through your body. That little voice on your shoulder telling you to pull that fucking trigger... Pull the fucking trigger bitch...

Dee pull that fucking trigger. You have all the power in your hands with a 357-auto automatic fully loaded and cocked to go. All of a sudden, nothing in that house matters. Not the fancy Clothes, Prada bags or Gucci shoes matter to you. Right now, a box on the street feels more like home, rather than the one you gave your soul and life to build.

Shit, you start thinking you should have been the one who laid each of those structural bricks. You should have been that plumber; you should be the one staying. However, your journey is over now, and instead of pulling that trigger, you turn around and walk away. I could have killed you that night, I caught you fucking my then best friend... yeah I knew about you fucking Kaliyah in that house on Washington Ave... and you called yourself saving me from my past... no nigga you just saving Kaliyah from me whooping her ass." My new relationship with Greg was a love hate type of thing.

"What? Damn Dee you are cold, you killed my baby? You was going to kill me. Damn that's cold..." I was starting to feel bad but relieved as he grabbed me from behind. I turned around and continued to talk... as we now stood face to face.

"Yes I aborted the baby, but you gave me every reason to... you fucked my best friend... and that son of hers is yours... Alison right?" I said as I pretended to cry for sympathy.

"Well while we are being honest... I busted several nuts in you that night we fucked after I came home. So I always wanted to ask you..." before we could finish our conversation... Kathy came rushing up the hill towards us... Just like a white girl in a movie she could not take leave me alone for an answer.

"Look that stunt you pulled in there worked I got so much information out of your mother, that could help us out. However, what you did to Bill was uncalled for... what did he do to you? Poor man is in so much pain." Kathy was showing me her crazy; I was not in the mood I was ready to give up.

"What did she say to you?" Greg questioned...

"Well for starters Jeff gay-thug ass is still alive... that's what she called him not me... poor girl couldn't kill her only living relative to her knowledge besides you Christa and Shawn. He lives in one of her houses she has in Philly or her old house... I don't know maybe it was property she still owns but she didn't say where..." Kathy confusedly stated; for a reporter, I thought she had done a horrible job dispatching her interview...

"Get the fuck out of here..." Greg flagged Kathy and started to walk away in disbelief, losing me in the mix...

"What do you mean Carlos and Antonio are on death row for killing him!" I mentioned...

"Well girly Melly said if you promise to come back and visit her she will tell you more about Mister Jeff herself." Kathy's smile was starting to look eerie.

"What do you mean if I come back to visit her, I have just a few hours left to find my daughter and husband alive... I don't have time to hear old family facts from an inmate who is flashbacking down memory lane."

"Look I kind of understand your agony, my father wasn't shit... my mother married different men to make ends meet, so there might be help for you, look I turned out alright."

"Fuck you Kathy you pulled one over on me... okay you owed me that after I sent you to Australia, but I don't owe you nothing else my bid with you is done." I replied...

"Look here girly we are already in too deep to go to the cops... especially since we don't have a story to back us up... it will look like we are the ones who are committing the wrongdoings, now besides with your luck you can't even trust the police."

"What do you mean?"

"I have to do more research, but I can't pair the pieces together with the smithereens we have on hand. We have to work together." Kathy had a point... "Let's go grab some brunch before we have to run from more cannonballs and shit...I need a V-8..." so since I was dumbstruck and naïve, I rolled on her suggestions, and I followed her lead. I never got the chance to finish my conservation with Greg.

Chapter 5

Criminal Minded

The diner was just a few miles down the road from the prison. I was not in the mood to eat; all I could do was wonder about my daughter. I sat across from Greg who sat next to Bridget, who sat across from Tim, who sat on the same side next to Terrace, and me while Bill and Kathy took the ends of the table and the other seat stayed empty.

Bill and Tim both ordered the steak and eggs with a side of grits. Kathy took the spinach omelet with provolone cheese. Terrance got pancakes, eggs and bacon. Bridget ordered a turkey burger and fries, while Greg and I both decided not to eat.

"How did Melly say Jeff was alive? What indication gave you the idea she was telling you the truth?" Greg asked out of nowhere considering the fact no one was talking to each other. Making our mixed crew look suspicious.

"She went on ranting after Christa stormed out in her hell fire of profane words."

"But what did she say word for word?" I asked...

"Well she mentioned Jeff being in the distribution house the same day Antonio so called raped her, and she rushed passed him. Therefore, he had to have known what Antonio did to her. Because my research from following your story, it is impossible for Carlos to keep his name up as a good cop if he offed Jeff himself. When Melly disappears so do Jeff, what did the man who took care of you look like if you can remember Christa?"

"Which one I was placed from home to home growing up before Mona and Antonio Jameson so called adopted me." I replied.

"Wait a minute.... This don't make since...!" Greg was not feeling Kathy's story just as much as I was not and between Kathy and Melly somebody was lying or Greg's truth was not true at all.

"I know Melly, and she just don't talk to just anybody and she don't tell on nobody. So who the fuck are you really and why are not calling the police on us? Don't you have an oath or something to follow? " Greg was starting to question Kathy's identity, reading my mind...

"Look I am who I say I am... I just want my story... I live for this reporter shit." Kathy was really showing her crazy... making herself questionable.

The table went silent; Greg and I both sat at the table staring at each other, while the crew was enjoying their meals. They was eating as if it was their last and this was our dying day. Neither Gee nor I was feeling the vibe. After all, it was our lives in danger and not to mention, my daughter and husband. Therefore, this eating without results shit was starting to annoy me on some real shit.

Consequently, without warning or fear of conflict, I got up and walked out of the door; when I walked, Greg was right behind me. I knew why he was on my top, but damn so fucking disrespectful to Bridget, not that I cared, but I did not know the facts of their situation.

"Get off of me..." I said in a soft tone of voice, struggling for him to let loose when he hugged me.

"I know I wasn't there for you then, but I will be damn if you will die in my arms, or if I was going to die in your arms... I would never put that on you and never would I want that feeling on me. I already lost you and that is hard to deal with. Do you really think I want to be stuck fucking random bitches all my life? None of these hoes can take your place.

You always been there for me no matter how much I shitted on you. I can at least be there for you, when you really need me there. You helped build me, although you left me during my turning point... I know I deserved that... but I will never forget the brand we built together... or the struggles in which we overcame. You been my day one and I owe you... Let's bounce shorty...

I picked pocked Bill and took the key to the truck. So it is either going to be me and you, or you and them! Because this shit we are facing is some real shit! I do not trust none of those motherfuckers, fuck that...and if they are whom they say they are; and ain't nobody paying them off; they are not built for this shit! So if you trust me... then on my move follow me..." I was sucker for his swag...

"But what if they follow or shoot after us?" Both Bill and Kathy had taken our guns, I said to myself... Greg didn't answer... On the count of three, Greg and I looked both ways then behind us... Then we ran like two thieves! We hopped into the truck; as fast as Greg could start the engine, we pulled out of the parking lot.

I could see Bill, Kathy and Tim chasing on foot behind us. I quickly stretched my leg over to the driver's side and pressed hard on Greg's foot. The gas pedal was on the floor. I was glad it was not the foot on the leg where I had shot him.

"Let go Dee I got this..." Greg shouted... I knew it must have hurt but I was terrified, I don't know why, but at this moment, Greg was the only one I knew I could trust or so I was anticipating.

"Dee do you remember where I used to park my other cars when I would pick up work from Omar and I would come up here to twist up my route?"

"Yes I remember why?"

"Because I still have a ride parked there and I have a house out there we can go for a second and get cleaned up... We cannot go on this ride looking like this... It won't look right."

"Okay..."

"Dee I got you, and you have my word I am not going to let anything happen to you. We are going to get out of this I promise."

"Okay..."

"I don't know about you, but I think Kathy was scheming you on some paid off shit. I do not know Bill's position in this but I am thinking he is running off anxiety. Terrance and Tim yah boys do not know these streets, and thugs ...whatever... they do not know the thugs we are dealing with... I feel bad Bridget ... Damn ..." Then Greg went mute.

"Who is Bridget?" I asked...

"Just a friend... That's it nothing more or less."

"Okay... So how long before we get to your house?"

"Not long..."

"Okay are you in on this and if so just blow me off now!"

"What...I meant what I said, I don't have nothing to do with this bull."

"This whole story just don't make sense to me... I mean all these twists and turns I am just over it."

"Look I couldn't tell you back then the things I was into, I just could not tell you everything. I can tell you now, I am no angel but I would never hurt a child or you... Melly and I took money from the distribution house and that was it. I do not know what other shit she did, I was still a young bull, I do not know all of what your mother was into. But something about Bridget isn't sitting well with me..."

"What about her that's your boo right?"

"I said a friend nothing more and nothing less but check this Dee... If this shit happened to you back then like the shit you pulled yesterday and all this shit going on now... How would you have been acting? And be for real..."

"Man I would have been going crazy trying to throw cash at everybody... hands in the air for real and by now me and her would have been fighting! I would have never sat so at eased with some who held me hostage... and I was disarmed... she should have went ham on me straight buck-wild."

"Right, now I know no two people act like in these situations but she ain't no regular jawn... Bee baby father is a big dope dealer her whole family sell dope... she didn't even plea life for us."

"So that don't mean she is about that life..."

"Naw shorty is about that life she carry a pistol in her purse and shorty just came home from doing a bid up north and shit. She be on some ride or die shit..."

"Damn Greg you still love them hood-rats. Maybe she was startled... I mean come on... lights out and guns to your head... all while you are butt naked; with a gangster who is balls deep inside of you..."

"Hood-rats need love too... you was a hood-rat when I first smashed you! Sike naw, but shorty bad and I cannot deny that... she might be a gutter buddy but I saw potential."

"Your mother was a hood-rat! So okay she choked so what..." He loved his baldheaded mother. His smart mouth was nothing I had missed. I hated that he threw everything he did for me, in my face.

"You keep my mom's name rolling off your tongue. Say it to her face and watch she drop you and I am going to laugh! Ain't no so what... That bitch is suspect too."

"Okay... so are you... Breast Milk!"

"Shit... On your life I am just as clueless as you are; believe that... and I know you didn't just call me a pussy..."

"I am just going to honest with you... I do not believe anyone... I just trust you right now because I know more about you then the rest... you can be in on this too... I just want to die knowing I tried to save my daughter and husband if I don't succeed."

"You are not going to die on me... I promise you my heart... You have are my word."

"So what are we going to do now?" I asked...

"Take matters into our own hands...I got to get this bullet out of my leg, I do know that... this shit hurt like hell."

"I am sorry I think..."

"It's the street code I understand; besides you probably been wanted to put a bullet in me..."

"Naw, maybe punch you in the eye or something but I never wanted to kill you..."

"Good to know, we are going to get the PT, nobody will believe the PT Cruiser, is us or suspect it for criminal intent. Not to mention the windows are tinted." How could he laugh at a time like this? I was nervous...

"What about the speed?"

"We don't need speed right now, that's one of the main things criminals look for in a target. They always bet on the other party to have so type of speed.... So no speed... we are going to creep up on these gutter goons."

"Sound crazy but okay..."

"Yo stop it with this okay to everything shit..."

"What okay..."

"So after we get cleaned up, we are going to head back to Philly. First, stop Plover Street, out Southwest. Then we hit up Maine Street out the county. Last stop Juniper and if we are lucky Bridge Street. You will drive and I will shoot if I have too."

Furthermore, while Greg was planning our plots I zoned out. I do not know what I was thinking about; I started imaging cows, and horses, running around a black and white field. The grass was lined in a maze like circle pattern. I could hear country music playing, and I was so hip-hop I do not know how I could hear something I never quite listen too... My mind was drifting... it was drifting. I could no longer see the road; all I could see was my wedding dress and me standing in it. With black lipstick on, and red hair draped over my shoulders. I was looking like the bride of Chucky.

My nails were painted white and razor sharp and super long. Thomas face was clear; the image of him looked invisible. I was tripping but I could not control it...I tried to sit with my head in the palms of my hands. I could feel my body shivering out of control...

"Dee what's good? Are you okay what is wrong with you? Baby talk to me, talk to me...." I could hear his voice but I could not speak... I was trying to get myself together, a picture of Mona flashed twice... and that is when I woke up.

"Dee are you cool don't be slipping on me..."

"Yeah I am good I am tired..."

"Are you sure? Well we can rest up a bit... I know you must be hungry..." Greg replied. On the other hand, all I could say was okay...

Chapter 6

Gas

Four-hour drive, after departing the diner in Cleveland, Ohio. Cincinnati, Cincinnati, Cincinnati ah freaking Cincinnati... I could not believe my eyes as Greg and I drove over the John A. Roebling Suspension, which runs over the famous Ohio River. It connects Covington Kentucky on the south bank of the Ohio River with Cincinnati. I did not remember Greg being the one who took me out here. I had been so many places with him, yet I could not recall freaking Cincinnati, with Greg.

We drove past the Embassy Suites at Cincinnati's River Center in Covington, Kentucky. Why were we all the way out there, I did not want to know, nor did I ask! I wanted to be surprised! This is not the plan... fucking fuck... was all I could think of, but I continued to be cool. Three blocks away for the hotel, we pulled into a parking garage. I counted the levels as we turned the corners. Four corners, so we must have stopped on the fifth, because the first floor did not have a corner.

"That's the car right there, you drive that one and follow me to dump this car..." Greg suggested.

"Where are the keys?" I asked...

"Oh you know feel under the frame of the tire on the driver's side." Following his orders, I got out of the truck and did as he said. I scrunched my eyes closed just in case he decided to shoot me in the back of my head and execute me. Once I got into the car, I reversed out of the parking spot and proceeded to follow him, exhaling a deep breath. After removing the trucks license plate and registration stickers and throwing them down a storm drain; another twelve blocks, we wiped the car clean, and drove it into a wooded area. With the engine still running, we watched as it rolled backwards off the cliff into a rushing body of water.

"Just me and my day one Bitch... game time baby... it's time to reload the game plan and beat these niggas at their own code of the streets... it's war let's get your daughter back... lets go get little baby girl..." Greg was back to plotting and I was back to being lost.

"What about my husband? We got to get him too..."

"Dee, yeah him too but baby girl first." All of a sudden, my phone ringed, I totally forgot I had it on my person... "What... no Dee don't tell me you still got that burner...." Greg quickly pulled to the side of the road in a frantic manner. "Get out of this car with that bull shit.... Tracers Dee, fucking tracers...." With his hands in the air, he let go of the steering wheel, puckering in frustration...

"What to do Greg I can't ... It's that number...." I yelled...

"Throw it away, roof that shit..." but instead of throwing it my heart answered it.

"Who are you?" I had to ask...

"Your worst fucking nightmare bitch, now tell me do you want your family back alive? Now my partner may have been soft on you but not me...the game you started to play with me; is going to get you murked. I am sorry I shot your friend, but hey can you blame me. You have my fucking money and I want my shit back. So tell me do you want your family?" I was trying to catch the tone of the voice but I could not, identify it...

"I don't have anyone's money mister, so tell me how do you know if, or what I have? Because it's obvious you know something about me that I don't know about myself... so stop playing your fucking game and tell me when and where I can come pick up my daughter and my mother fucking husband... then tell me how many fucking bullets you want in your fucking head.

I do not give a fuck about how big of the big bad wolf you are... I did nothing to you, now it would be different if you told me who the fuck are you.... Pussy and meet me face to face like a fucking boss... I am tired of playing this fucking rat-race with you... this shit is drawling and I am so fucking over it... if you want my blood then bitch come get it..." forget being Christa... Dee was back... I was feeling pumped.

"How cute little girl, your rebellious toddler temper is not going to raddle my feathers or my reason as to why I am after you and Greg... so if you really want your husband and your brat back... I suggest you pay attention. I am not in any type of mood to play games with you either. Bitch did you think it would be that easy to destroy an empire, I worked hard to build? Funny you are just another silly hoe with a price on her head... fifty million, and I am petty I like my bills broken up and all faced... don't plan on cheating me either; I count mine before handing over..."

"Who tagged my head?" I questioned trying to keep him on the line long enough to catch his voice.

"Don't worry about that sweetheart... you have three days to show your ratting ass face... oh and don't forget my money.... I will call you in two and a half days to tell you where we will meet..."

"Wait don't hang up, proof first that my family is alive...."

"Your pretty face wants to speak to you my friend..." the voice, replied...

"Deandra it's me... Thomas... what is going on?" this time I was for sure of the voice, and my heart melted in the blank of that second...I sat on the receiver speechless... I never heard Thomas sob before... this shit was real.

"I am coming baby..." Then I hung up... I got back into the car with Greg, and as we pulled off, I wrote down the number the kidnapper was calling me from, and then I tossed the phone out of the window.

"What did he say?" Greg asked...

"Fifty million dollar bounty on our heads, he put Thomas on the phone.... and he called me pretty face after he called me a bitch." I point out.

"Pretty face, so he knows you?"

"I don't know him though what makes you think he know me?"

"Fifty million dollar bounty on your head and he calls you pretty face... so he wants you to bring him the cash in order for him to give you back Journey and Thomas. But this shit don't make any sense... what if Thomas is the one doing all of this, because them niggas Melly and I fucked with would have banged them already... where did you meet boul at any way?"

"My husband has his own money... it's not Thomas..."

"Well until we figure this shit out he is suspect too... this shit don't make sense to me...my goons... my goons... I don't know... why they would say it was me when they contacted you. On the other hand, who is on this nut shit... you know me I straight go get mines and so do every other baller I know. I be in the hood, they could have confronted me there. However if you had my money... all honesty you would have been gave me my money.... On my life real shit... the only reason why I got your back now Dee is because I want to know who sent you after me... and at the end of the day I fucks with you heavy... you will forever be my bitch...I ride for those who ride with me... You feel me..."

"Yes I know, thank you..."

"It's cool baby girl lets go get cleaned up and load these units up and ride out like crack babies and tear these streets up my way..." I loved when Greg gave me my assurance that I could trust him. I admit I never stopped loving him...

We pulled up to his one- story, ranch style home, in the middle of bubble fuck, yet just outside of Cincinnati's downtown. I really did not remember this trap house. Greg must have me mixed up with one of his other girls... the inside looked like a regular house nothing to jump up and down over, I wasn't missing anything not remembering that place.

Light brown wood panel walls, tan carpet throughout the house. A regular kitchen with regular white appliance's, even an old floor model television sitting in the dining area. I was not surprised to see Greg reaching into the brick frame of the house to remove the keys and a small pistol. He always had slick places to plant keys and things in case of an emergency. I entered the house feeling alleviated. While Greg searched the entire house looking for intruders and signs of changes with his petite gun in hand. I forgot how living like this felt… and not even for a minute did I miss it.

"Its clear baby girl, are you hungry?"

"Starving…" I replied

"Cool I was just up here about a week ago, good thing I went shopping, it's some frozen pizza in the fridge and a couple of TV dinners."

"A week ago, what for?"

"Business had to pack my nickel-rocks, and relax…"

"Oh so are you sure we are safe here?"

"Yeah don't nobody but you know about this trap house."

"You keep saying I been here before but that's not true I don't remember this place…"

"You don't? We came here before; it's been years though…" Greg replied before walking away to go heat up the food.

"Hey I can do it, do you have anything to get that bullet out?" I decided to take over the cooking. I wanted to know everything that was going into the food.

"Okay yeah, I have a first aid kit in the bathroom, you know you have to pull it out…"

"Me?" oh I hated blood I thought to myself…

"Stop being a punk yeah you…" he replied laughing…

"Whatever okay…"

Then within seconds after placing the food into the oven, Greg returned with his first aid kit and took a seat on the ugly green plaid couch. I could not help but to grunt my teeth when he took off his pants. I do not know how I could think about having a sexual flashback in a situation like this but damn my feelings for Greg were starting to return. Thomas and Journey… I kept saying to myself, while thinking damn…

I was glad to see the bleeding had stopped, that was a good sign I hit no arteries. Nevertheless, the wound was crusty. First, I checked for an exit wound; it was just godsend there was one; right above the backside of his knee. I could see the bullet pushing out of his leg. Therefore, after having turned Greg flat on his stomach, I poured fresh water over the wound to wash it clean. I then wiped the tweezers with rubbing alcohol to sterilize them.

I removed a bullet out of his hand once, so that the police would not be able to trace the bullet after he gone to the hospital. However, this time was different, I could not get the bullet out and I was petrified to try again because it had broken in half.

"Greg it broke, I can't get it. You are going to have to go to the emergency room…" I said crying out for him to tell me to stop.

"Naw we are in too deep, fill the spray bottle up with water and I will spray while you pinch and squeeze the rest of the bullet out. Double up your gloves..."

"What.... But it's going to hurt Greg you can die from the metal..." I cried out...

"Dee you shot me, okay you have my word I am not going to die in your arms ... okay so just hurry up and do it..." Damn his crazy ass was serious I thought to myself, so I did it.

It took me five tries before the bullets tail came gushing out, and quickly I grab a gull and covered the wound with pressure. Next, I cleaned out the laceration with a mix of hydrogen peroxide and the sterilizing solution that was in the kit. Slowly I pushed the threaded needle into Greg's leg and started sewing him up. Twelve stiches in the exit and six in the opening. My stitch work looked professional, I made sure to zigzag the thread. By the time, I was finish cleaning up Greg's leg, the food smelled done. We washed our hands and took a seat at the table; as if everything we had just done was normal.

We ate in silence, I was feeling numb, and was trying to forget what I had just done. Greg on the other hand was a born thug he was custom to this crap. After finishing our chicken breast TV-diners, I cleaned up the kitchen; then as Greg took a seat on the couch I went into the bathroom to shower... as the water ran hot, I undressed and got in, drenching my entire body including my hair. I stood there for about fifth-teen minute's day dreaming and praying. I am guessing the smell of the Dove soap surfed under the bathrooms door and into the nose of Greg. I jumped, when the shower curtain opened. I did not hear the door open, even though I had been listening with open ears. I turned around and he was completely nude. Speechless I gawked, for a moment.

"One last time... can I have one last time...?" Greg said looking filthy sexy...

"What? Greg I am married..." I replied dropping the bar of soap. Then without words, Greg climbed into the shower with me...

"Wash my back and let me wash yours..." He answered back... and then again, without words, I switched places with him and faced him to the water to wash his body. In return, he respectfully washed mine. I hurdled when he tried to take the rag and clean my private parts.

"Just my back Greg..." I spoke in a soft tone of voice. Knowing I wanted to wrap my legs around him and explode in ecstasy...

I cannot lie it felt blameless to be in this position with him. I had missed this side of our friendship. After the shower, I went into the bedroom to get dress. He gave me one of his cotton sweat suits to dress in, but I wanted the jeans so he gave me the jeans. I could fit his pants after all; his slim waist was as slim as mine was. When I bent over to pull up the jeans from the bottom to squeeze them up over my hips, Mr. Weston decided to come and stand behind me. As I than stood up straight, he put his hands around my waist and whispered...

"One last time... can I have one last time?" the rumble of his voice slow speaking through his Adams apple quivered my body into overdrive. I wanted Greg's penis to thrush against my vaginal walls and pound me... nonetheless, my daughter was all I could ponder about...

"No sex is the last thing racing through my mind." I replied then I walked into the other direction and took a seat on the other side of the bed. As I slid, the pants up and pulled the black tee shirt over my head. I had washed my bra and underwear and sat them over the shower rod, to dry. I was bare bottom and top loose when, Greg decided to slide behind me on the bed. He grabbed me by my waist the way I am guessing he had remembered I adored. He then slid his head right into my lap body hugging me hard enough to make me fall onto him.

When I tried to get up, he pulled me tighter. Then he started licking my earlobe; making my nipples get hard. Greg's teasing was stimulating my power of having self-control. I noted my sexual wants by pressing my butt into his pelvis. I then tugged at his undershirt before I took my hands and reached into his boxer shorts. Swiping my fingers to strike at his gun sausage. I couldn't hold on to my marital vows yet again. I had not cheated on Thomas with Greg since the day we had gotten married. When I met up with him in Cali, we did not have sex.

The last time I had unprotected sex with Greg was the day before all of that shit went down with the FED's. In the back of my mind, I often wondered if Thomas was really Journey's father.

My baby has no genetic evidence her father is a pure African; except for the fact she picked up his native accent, being though his homeland is where I had been raising her. I also had sex with Cory, Greg's brother; the same night he finally let me work for him. That was the only reason why he did not tell Greg I was booty popping in his private rooms.

I felt betrayed when I found Greg in bed with my best friend. Although me sleeping with his brother happened after Greg had come home from jail, and the affair Greg and Kaliyah happened before he went to jail. Karma has no statute of limitations as to when she is coming back to fuck you in your footsteps. I never wanted to find out the truth about the father of my daughter. If it was truly, a white lie... I was taking that white lie to the grave with me.

Thomas was the perfect daddy for her. He was legally rich and successfully established. Making Journey heir to the throne. Besides that, I did not want to know, because I knew how I felt when I found Kaliyah's son paternity test in her purse. Ninety- nine point –nine percent... Gregory Weston was the father of then one- year old Makhi Geovanni Jones-Weston. I could have strangled her in the car that day; Greg choked the guard in the prison after we was caught having sex in the restroom.

Instead, I got so drunk at the bar with Kaliyah hoping to obliterate my pain and my mental state of mind. However when Greg threw Alison in my face, I seethed in anger towards him. I aborted what would have been my third child by him. I destroyed most of his empire. I sold all of his cars that I knew about, and burnt all of his clothes. When Greg came home, he had to start over with his extravagant things. I purposely left him twenty-dollars, from the money I had control over; if I had access to the accounts he had in my name at the time... empty I would have left them. I guess he had other savings, because he was back on his feet within weeks, after his release from jail.

As I rolled over thirsting, horny, moaning, and groaning, rodeo grinding. I pulled the tee shirt over my head and excepted Greg apple bobbing on my breast. I swiveled my hips in a circular motion, slow winding on him. Then he flipped me over and before he could bottom-top me I removed my pants. In the same period, he removed his plaid boxers and thrashed his man-hood on my womanly peek.

I exhaled and pushed it inside of me. I was thinking this was my twenty-four hours to live. I loved intimacy it was the only thing that made me feel secured. It was the only sense of comfort I knew. I had a thing for scratching backs so I scratched his back and pulled at the sheets. Intercourse with Greg was different then sex with Thomas. I always wanted to conjure a mix of the two. Thomas was a Mandingo lovemaking machine. While Greg on the other hand, was a ghetto freaky untamed animal perfectly average in size and width.

Greg made me feel young again. However, I felt like Deandra when I was with him. On the other hand, Thomas made me feel like a queen, the princess Melly said I was to her. However, Thomas was controlling; his hands became short tempered. I always said I wanted to walk the streets feeling like me, but I was a person, I never had a chance to know. I loved the non-street life I got from Thomas, but I yarned for the fight I got from Greg. Consistently called beautiful was darling majority of the time, but I missed being called a bad bitch. Thomas was just too good and too bad to love; but I loved his deeds. The beatings with his belts had to stop. I wanted to walk away but I would have been broke and stuck. I didn't know how to stand on my own. I feared of losing everything. I was more scared of being broke, then I was falling to the ground because of his hand.

I was pivoting in my thoughts all while rodeo riding this untamed animal. Thinking please Greg have mercy on me, so much pain tied up into so much dirt. Damn he was pumping me with gas. Not only did I smell it but also I felt it slide down the crack of the buttock and on to the sheet that was still under me. I knew there was nothing I could do about it. I was feeling the moment, I just knew I could not forget about it, if and when this headhunter storm was over and the bounty was off my head.

Part 3

Igniting the fire

I slept in another man's arms that evening for the first time in months. I met up with Omar about a year ago, when Taylor first sold her side of the story to the media. It was not my intentions to make him a number on my gynecology record. We just so happened to be on vacation in St. Thomas the same time; I was there with Thomas celebrating our anniversary. Omar was there with some friends. I was guessing he was celebrating his release from prison; he got out of jail two years after Greg.

When I saw him by the poolside being water whipped by the loose women reggae dancing for his friends and his attention. At first, I thought I should hide my face. I even thought about leaving the island, and persuading Thomas to come along. However, instead of hiding I brought attention to myself, hoping me ground dancing in front of my husband; as if I was, a drunken slut would point his eyes into my direction.

Omar was flexing that jailhouse glow, most men get while serving time in the pin. My seductive dance moves worked in my favor. When he turned my way, I knew he had noticed me. I was not looking to sleep with Omar; I just wanted to get some information out of him. He and I had been cool. I lost touch with him after Greg came home. Greg no longer allowed me, to put my nose into his commerce or his friend's commerce. I went back to my lane and stayed there, minus marrying my way out of being Greg's main chick, into unholy matrimonial bliss.

Even though I felt like I had burnt the shit that use to hurt... I had a lot of unfinished business to resolve. That next morning while Thomas went on his two-hour workout along the beach trail. I opted not to go, blaming my late night drinking the reason why I did not want to work out with him. My husband was controlling he left my body guard Martin outside of the door of our penthouse suite.

Martin was a big buff sweetheart; I knew he had been working overtime, so I used his needs to compliment mine. Relieving him from his duties I assured him, I was good. I told him, to walk me down to the lobby restaurant for breakfast, instead of me ordering room service, incase Thomas was still hanging around in the building.

I had noticed Martin had made a new friend, whom was also there with a group of friends. It would have been impossible for him to enjoy his trip, Thomas made sure security protected, us at all times. Thomas and his family was high-profile people in his country. After all, they were one of the wealthiest families living there. I pre-wrote my number on a tiny piece of paper anticipating to slip it into Omar's hands.

The only blessing over breakfast was Martin invitation to pussy prowl on the third floor. Everyone knows luck like that do not get two calling calls. For that reason, I told him to take his chances. White girls love to Eiffel tower black men in porns. What a lucky dog he was and an empty ditz I became. After Martin departed the elevator onto the third floor with his spring break freaks, I stayed on to mope back up to the ocean view penthouse, to think of another master plan. Then when The Ritz-Carlton's, elevator's door opened on the fifth floor, I got off passing Omar on purpose.

Then on purpose, he bumped me. I turned around without saying a word. I continued to walk down the hallway. As if, I was going to my room, but I was on the wrong floor, so I kept walking, good thing the floor turned into a circle. I could hear footsteps walking behind me, when I glimpsed over my shoulders; it was Omar following me, and his crew was long gone up the elevator. Maybe they were going to the rooftop for the day party I thought.

"Hey stranger..." Omar called to me from behind. I turned around hoping his hello was friendly.

"Do you know me?" I said pretending to act as if I forgot who he was.

"Don't act like you don't know me Dee, how can you forget Omar?" he gestured in laughter.

"Oh shit stop playing wow how long has it been?" I replied while reaching out to give him a hug. Of course, he hugged me back smelling good.

"Yeah I know I just got out a few weeks ago, I am out here on business you know." He then responded.

"No I had not talked to your boy in a minute; I am on my own now. I got married four years ago; I am done with that Gee life." I commented trying to sound like a changed woman.

"I heard you crushed my man heart! What's up with him though do yall still keep in contact?"

"Not really, I changed numbers and zip codes on him."

"Oh really wow, what happened?"

"The love faded he want to do him the way he knows how. I guess we outgrow each other." I said lying because I knew the two of them was still homie's; and I knew I had just met up with Greg in New York, a few months before I stopped speaking to Taylor for good. Even though Greg and I met on business, I did not sleep with him.

"Did he really move to Connecticut? The last time I saw him he was talking about moving up there!" Strange I thought they were best friends... Greg always told people he live in downtown Philly, and he didn't tell others his moves. Shit he didn't even tell me things until the day it happened and after the fact.

"I don't know when I talk to him it's just to say hi. I don't ask him about his business anymore." I said thinking to myself... the only person besides me who knew about Alpine was Melly I was assuming. I knew Omar didn't know before, therefore I was not telling him.

"I hear that... so what's up?" Omar asked...

"Enjoying my vacation... It was good seeing you, happy to know you are alright." I said smiling my pearly whites.

"So why are you looking for me on the fifth floor? You are in the penthouse right?"

"I was not looking for you Omar!" Damn, I thought, he was still good at his game.

"Really, what you was scared I might do something to you on the elevator?"

"Scared why should I be sacred of you? Do we have beef I don't know about?" I questioned.

"Yeah we have beef!" he said smiling...

"What? Don't start no shit with me Omar... my husband is bigger and crazier than you!"

"Ah fuck your husband Dee, what time can I steal you for lunch?"

"Lunch bye boy... why would I go to lunch with you?" I asked why when I should have been asking how...

"Ask your pootang that... that cooter been asking for me to jam-rock it!"

"Get the fuck out of here... what's up with your wife Keliney?" I said being smart...not knowing if he know her as Melly in real life or if he know she was my mother...

"Nothing she was never my wife... she left me remember! Gee and his crazy ass friends. That girl stole my money and my heart. I can't wait to find her ass... Gee thought that shit was funny, he hasn't seen her either. We don't know where that girl ran off too..." Then he smiled again...

"You are crazy boy... what do I look like smashing the homie?" I replied all while following him down the hall and around the corner to his room. Although Thomas was well off and I had access to his funds, I enjoyed making my own income. Omar put what looked like a stack into the waistband of my shorts. I was far from a prostitute; I never sold myself for money. However, I never took off my panties and returned home with just a wet ass either. Door locked and curtains closed; I flushed my water over Omar's pipe.

"You are a bad bitch I tell you!" Omar whispered, while he hammered me in his arms against the wall.

"You are strong!" I whispered back into his ear. I had been suffering from depression I missed my ghetto attention. Being Mrs. was staring to take a toll over me. Goodie good shoes was boring. I was mad at the past; therefore, I let it fuck me in the future... My whorish habits I never burnt. There is a saying I used to know...

"Whores who turn into house wives dies slow..." the realist quote ever because although I was happy in wealth with Thomas my needs for feeling free was limited, and beaten; I was torn. They say hurt people; hurt people... we both were hurt people. Yeah I had freedom to sleep good at night; but I did not have freedom to live free. I had gone straight from living in Greg's footsteps to walking into Thomas's honor. Omar gave me my own income, so I continued to meet up with him, months after our St. Thomas reunion. My affair with Omar ended a few months before this bullshit had started. Things between us was starting to get too adjacent to home for my wellbeing.

My husband had signed a business contract with my then him-stress. I knew Omar was drug money; however, Thomas knew him as discounted trade. Otherwise his labor union manager. Omar's people cleaned Thomas's hotels in the United States, mostly in Florida, Texas, California, and Arizona... the human trafficking states.

Chapter 7

Prohibited by law

I woke up not on ecstasy feeling more like crap, one thing on my mind and that was to save my daughter. The headache I had embraced a day ago was still pounding at my head. I was down to follow the street rules and go against the rules the economy was to live by. Looking into Greg's eyes as we sat at the table in the basement of the house cataloguing out the bullets and guns. If I did not know Greg, I would have though he was some sort of street terrorist or head of the CIA! From hand grenades to A-k47's, sniper weapons, swords, bulletproof vests... ropes and all kinds of killer shit. I was mind blown yet feeling so much like Mona.

Greg passed me my favorite pistol a 357-automatic, and a Smith and Wesson. It was the first gun he taught me how to shoot when I was fifth-teen. Heavy duty for a girl like me but forever my favorite. When he gave me my vest, I strapped it on skintight. Once the both of us was dressed and equipped for the worst, we carried two duffle bags each to the car, and placed them into the back seat. Dressed in all black, common was the look we was going for.

Going after vengeance under the street code could be very dangerous yet complicated. Still I was not one-hundred percent sure Greg was the person I should have been trusting with my life. He was still an enemy I could call to the eye of the gun. I was not religious but I was praying to see my baby's eyes again and feel her touch one more time.

Pulling out of the driveway, I took the first set of hours heading back to Philly. What seemed like a long ride to Cincinnati, seem like a shorter ride back to Philly; and just like planned unannounced we loaded our guns and started checking the street runners off the list. First stop was right off the inter-state I95 ramp in Southwest Philly. We stopped for gas, and then proceeded to our destination on Plover street. A small block tucked right behind the busy rail station tracks.

It was a small suburban house, Melly owned and I never knew she had. If we had kicked in the door, the thumping noise would have alarmed the neighbors. Therefore, we stalked the house until nightfall, and under the moons glow after seeing no movement in the home, the tip of our screwdriver gave us access to the inside. What seemed to be a nicely kept home on the outside was sweltering in the horrifying smell of a body rotting!

There was no other sign of forced entry from what we could tell. I covered my nose with my free hand while my other hand had the gun. Room by room we searched police watching one another's backs. The first floor was clear, but blood trailed up the wall to the second floor. As we climbed the steps, we could both see a hand hanging over the landing through the banister.

It was the body of a man, who looked to be in his forties and well-manicured for a man's touch. His facial hair been waxed and he was wearing foundation, fake eyelashes and coral pink lipstick. Melly's name was still on the deed of the house, but who was this freak that was gut- shot in the hallway, of her two-story three bedroom house. Things like this was strange for the side of town.

"Who is that, do you know him?" I questioned...

"No, but it must have gotten real around here, something is up..." Greg replied as he started checking the pockets of the dead man's clothes.

"Don't get any blood on you, we don't need nothing tracing back to us..." I replied... petrified that this shit was getting out of control... thinking to myself I never wanted this crap to get this deep.

At that, moment as the two of searched the rest of the rooms, before we left I decided to look at the pictures that were on the walls, and on the living room tables. There was a picture of me when I was little, standing alongside Melly. I stashed the small frame with the photo in it, into the waist of my pants. Then as I continued to look, I noticed Melly had taken a picture of me the day that I met her, in New York; at the house Omar and she had together. I took that photo as well. Then as soon as I got finished stuffing the pictures into my pants, Greg came rushing out of the basement.

"Come on let's go we have to get out of here!" He said holding a grocery store plastic bag, with stacks of money in it...

"Where did you get that from?" I asked him, looking at him sideways...

"Down stairs, come on lets go, I will explain it to you once we get out of here baby girl."

The night sky was starting to fade away, as the two of us exited through the back door. We crept back to our car, which we had parked two blocks away from the house. Greg took over the steering wheel of the car until we stopped a mile away from his trap house on the other side of Southwest Philly.

"You drive, and do what I tell you to do..." Greg demanded...

"What are you about to tell me to do now? You haven't even said two words to me yet about where you got that bag of money from and why you took it." Damn I thought to myself, thinking about what did I get myself into...

"Dee, just do what I tell you to do..." Greg said as he pulled out his gun and sat it on his lap.

"Okay what do you what me to do Greg? Drive or sit here?"

"Drive regular, and watch your mirrors for the cops..." I did what he told me to do, and I turned where he said turn...

"Slow down and turn the lights out..." Greg said as he rolled down his passenger side window... "When I say go... drive faster...," he added...

King Street was a small side block; I used to ride though looking for Greg, back in the days. Never could I imagine being the getaway driver in a drive by shooting, hosted by Greg himself. There was two women and three men standing outside near the corner of the block... they never had a chance to draw their guns if they had any on them, and they never had the chance to run either.

Greg shot them with his automatic that he pointed out of the window... and as he kept pulling the trigger, the bodies kept falling. I never wanted to get this deep involved. I just wanted to find my baby, and husband alive... damn is this what being greedy feels like I thought as I quivered.

I drove straight off of King Street, and hopped onto the highway. I got off the exit in South Philly we dumped the car in a parking lot near Center City with the doors unlocked and the engine running. We knew within seconds of us leaving the car unattended, that some carjacker would come steal it. I was starting to take notice that Greg had cars parked all over the city in random places. The more I started noticing things about him that I did not know before, the more I was getting timid.

Greg drove us to the far end of the Northeast; we sat parked in a wooded area, near a train station. I don't know what time I had closed my eyes I was exhausted. Jumping up from out of my sleep, I must have scared Greg; he too jumped, reaching for his pistol that was laying in his lap.

"Don't shoot it's just me Greg..." I shouted out...

"What the fuck are you jumping for?" he replied...

"Nothing, where are we?" I questioned...

"In bubble fuck..."

"Stop playing what is going on Greg you are scaring me..." Greg still was not talking to me...

"Look, what did the person who called you say on the phone to make you think it was me?"

"I told you everything, so tell me what and why you are shooting people for nothing..."

"Nothing I did was for nothing baby girl, let me tell you something... there are rules to the streets, however these rules are coded. Now I have been in this game my whole life. I started from the bottom; and once you get to the top... players try to give you options. It is almost impossible for someone in my position to come home from jail and still have his or her position. The rules is to kill the king and take his spot or option two... push him out and take his spot. They rather see you in jail or in the streets somewhere six feet deep.

Dee, I re-wrote the code of the streets. When I came up with Pete, I changed the game. I made the dope game on the East Coast what it is, I feed these dope dealers and their families. Therefore, I am thinking since these players want me they must not be hungry. One thing I do not like is the ungrateful... the difference between Carlos and me, is I did my own time... I never asked any of my men to take any of my charges. I am a man and I am king of this throne. I control everything drug related in this city.

Last night, I shot up my distribution house. King Street belongs to me. The code of the streets first rule is not to disturb home. Every hustler knows not to bring no drama to King Street. Since the person who is going through you to get me is asking for money, as if they know me, then if they are smart they will know I cannot get to the money because King Street is hot now. This will buy us some time on narrowing our options. I wonder if your people Kathy and them called the cops by now... because baby girl... This bullshit do not add up. Why would a reporter. Try to bull-rate us at gunpoint.

I mean, she was the only person who could get you close to Philly; I have known you your whole life; I did nothing to you but love you... and even still I had to meet you out in Cali! You stopped coming to New York to meet me... why Dee... Is there anything you want to tell me now before this shit gets deeper than what it is; because this shit is senseless, I am starting to feel like I am running for nothing...? I have been in this game my whole life and never, never have I had to go on a duck hunt like this before."

"So what's next? And why did you take that money out of Melly's house, where did you get it from?" I questioned...

"Oh, I got from the basement that was my money... why did you take her pictures?" he replied in a sarcastic tone of voice.

"Why was your money in her house?"

"Because I put it there..."

"Hold up so do you know that he-she?" oh shit I thought to myself...

"Yeah I know him that was him..." Greg said laughing while showing me a photo he pulled from his pocket, of a man that was dressed like a woman...

"He looks familiar..."

"Carlos boy... faggot ass Jasper... he don't come around the hood that often... Carlos keeps him on a hush. Melly don't even know him..."

"Who shot him... was it you...?"

"You really think I am some kind of killer hun?"

"I didn't say that... I am just..."

"Just what... yeah I shot him! Is that what you are trying to figure out... you want me to confess... to you..."

"I am just asking I don't want to get any deeper into this..."

"Deeper, baby girl shut up you sound stupid, if you didn't want to get deep into this shit, then you should have never came looking for me... let me explain something to you... I am a gangster I do gangster shit..."

"Greg just tell me what is going on, is my family still alive?"

"I told you love I don't have your family, Jasper and I had some beef and I ended it...that's what that shit was about..."

"But why Melly house? What do she have to do with it...?"

"Why are you worried about Melly, your mother is a thug baby girl, she is a drug dealer... why not her house... some shit went down, he intruded on private property. Melly is still my right hand, I am sorry..."

"Wow, so why did you go back to the house?"

"To get my money! Look I am going have to meet with my team in a minute, I am sure word got out about the distribution house shooting. It's still early, the shift didn't change yet... but I know the streets are talking." I just sat there lost for words.... Thinking damn. This motherfucker is insane... what fool would go back to a crime scene, when he could have got the money the same day he shot dude. My mind was going out of control.

Just like clockwork six in the morning on the dot, Greg phone started ringing... the first call he sent to voice mail... the second call went to voice mail... the fifth call he picked up...

"What's up...?" he answered...

"Lies..." he responded to the voice on the other end of phone...

"King Street, who was out there?"

"No way, damn how hot is the block?" I was trying to hear what the caller was saying to him but the volume on his phone was low...

"Round up the heads get all my men off the streets... the store is closed today, until further notice... I want all the Captains to meet me at lipstick at noon sharp... Co- captains are to take charge from this point."

"No I'm not around, who?" then he looked at me...

"Oh really, naw tell me in person you doing too much talking over the phone..." then he ended the call...

"Why are you looking at me like that...?" I questioned...

"No reason, I love you Dee... why did you go get married on me... your eyes I love them..." Greg replied as he reached over to kiss me... I kissed him back then I pushed him...

"What do you mean why did I get married, where did that come from..."

"Nowhere, this shit is crazy baby girl... love and the street code don't mix... shit is out of control love... I hope I can help you... you know I will do anything for you. Anything for you..."

"Wow I still have that privilege..."

"You never lost it; you just went and married that plum-purple looking dude on me... I am not mad at you, jealous maybe...but I don't blame you... to be honest... I am over this street life... I really been chilling other than that jezebel minding my business. It is just hard to leave... it's not the money anymore, I made that; it's just these nigga's they do not know how to let a nigga be great. It is like you are damned if you do, and damned if you don't... if I let the game go easy they will think I am sitting on bigger numbers then what I am sitting on, and they are going to want it... you can't get the type of chicken change I am getting and not collect enemies.

This chicken change got everybody and his or her mother looking for the right time to come after me. Do you really know what it feel like not to be able to trust nobody? I do, other than you... I can't trust nobody; not even Melly can't be trusted; as much as I respect her as a person."

"Why me?" I asked...

"Why not you, the love I have for you is real, just because I am a gangster, does not mean that I don't have feelings. I do have feelings... I am human. Besides I love you that's why... and you still love me..."

"I do love you..."

"But what?"

"I am scared Greg, I love that little girl with my heart..." I replied as I bust out into tears...

"Look I know, that is why I am going to help you get her back... I have to go to this meeting, let's go get some breakfast, and change this car." Greg said as he started the car and drove to a used car parking lot that was located along the Boulevard. There we changed cars yet again. He picked out a black Jeep.

"How many cars do you have and why are they parked all over the city..." I questioned...

"I have a lot of them, you never know when somebody is going to try to at you... in this game you have to be ready, I've seen so many players go down from not being prepared... call me paranoid... but I own a couple of car lots...we cool..." With his fitted hat turned to the back, swag turned on... I was beyond scared. I hated when he talked like this, making the bad seem so cool.

"Paranoid for real..." I repeated...

"Shit the streets do more than talking they watch too! For that, I have to watch my back! You have to be clever the street code is not the same, anymore." The calming of Greg's tone of voice was scaring the be Jesus out of me, I felt like he knew something, and the something was the side I was not telling him. It was as if he was reading me but not understanding me; I drove Greg to Lipstick, the club Cory still owned on the back road near the Airport. Cory no longer used Lipstick for a strip club; Cory had moved his club to Center City. I guess he got exhausted after the club was shut down, due to the drug dealers trapping.

Chapter 8

Snake Fishing Through the Eyes of Greg

Someone once asked me, "where do I see myself ten years from now?" the streets always been home for me; some who ask questions, don't understand; I was raised in this business. I've seen the good of it, and I've witness the worst of it. Nothing in the middle matters, the middle is the struggle. Even when I was locked –up, I was still relevant within the streets. Learning from the forerunners, and the ones I rocked with and the ones I heard about; attention was the most valuable bill I ever had to pay for...

Paying attention was more important than graduating high school, it was more important than anything in my world that I could learn. Personality traits, body language, trigger words, the blurred lines; I had to memorize them and I had to learn them, you know sort out the good and the evil. I am the definition of a hustler; and with my hustler mentality shine the gangster.

Ten years before to the date, I could not answer that question. When I was in prison for two years, doing the longest bid I ever had to do, a close friend of mine came to visit me. Dee always thought I was lying about Alison, I think Dee wanted to believe Alison was really Kaliyah. Truth was I had babies by both Kaliyah and Alison, while I was dealing with Dee. Kaliyah son is older and if Dee had kept, the second child she aborted by me their kids would have been the same age. At that time in my life, I didn't want children; Dee was too egotistical to be any body's mother; and the way I was trapping, I never wanted the streets to take them from me. The way I loved Dee was enough, and losing her would have been enough. I had enough...

I never cared for Kaliyah she was a loose goose! Who in the hood didn't pop her? She used to hang out in my trap house on Washington Ave, with one of my corner boys Stanley; that was his girl. When he got booked, shorty needed money to bail him out that was her job not mine. I always told the hoppers to make sure they put some money up in a place someone they loved could get to it and bail them out. Some listened and a lot of them didn't. Me being the man that I am, I let her pay his debts off; cleaning and cooking for my team, packing weight and things like that. I did not have Dee that close into what or whom I was doing business with; Dee made major moves with me and for me, but not everything was for her to know.

I am not going to lie Kaliyah's body was bad... big tits a rump shaker and she wasn't ugly either.

Being alone one day with her in the house, one thing led to another, we went from working, to talking; in the mist of her sucking me off, things got out of hand. I am guilty for allowing things to go where they went I really felt offal. All it took was that one time, and she popped up pregnant. I was like didn't you just have a baby? That creep is not mine... and if you think it is mine; you are not having it... I am not doing shit for it bitch... I begged her to get rid of it... she straight up told me ..."No..."

Kaliyah burnt me several times, one second she was down for it, then the next she was like fuck you and Dee. I gave her about three-thousand dollars to terminate that baby. I personally took her to the clinic to get it done. She came out the room talking about I can't do this... it took everything out of me not to push her back into that office and hold her legs open my damn self.

Shit I even thought about offing her. Her mindset was like "jackpot". However, I did not know what would hurt Dee more; finding out I offed her friend or finding out I had a baby with her friend. Me being a man I figured, Dee would learn to forgive me as she had done on two other occasions; when she found out I slipped cheating. Shit Dee went with me to take them girls to get rid of theirs! Steam blowing out of her ears Dee sat in the room with them. I knew Dee and the Dee I knew, would have killed both Kaliyah and me no questions asked. I turned that girl into a pit-bull. Dee was mean when I started fucking with her, but with me being a piece of work, I turned her into something else.

Twenty-thousand not to tell Dee or nobody else I was the father. Another ten-thousand to stay away from me, and one-thousand a week every Friday for pampers and things. I did not sign the birth certificate; I did not go to the hospital when she had him; I did not know his name. She told me and I forgot that shit on purpose. I was not trying to be no father, she was a day party stand, I never spent no nights with her sexually... she was nothing to me, and I wanted her to feel that. I took Dee from her, her only friend; I made Dee turn her back on her... or so I believed...

Welfare took me to court, Kaliyah wanted food stamps and child support, when I got locked-up. That Hood-rat signed my name on her child's birth certificate. I was in jail dealing with my own shit, I get some mail and the courts was serving me papers. DNA test came back ninety- nine point nine percent little nigga mine; Makhi Geovanni Jones-Weston, she gave him my last name. Alison asked me "Why Dee, what is it about Dee that I can't leave alone?"

Alison was a good girl with no ties to the streets. I met her one day at the mall; she did not know me, and I did not know her. Alison was in college studying at the University of Penn; but she was from California. We became close friends, she

86

was someone I could talk regular to without her judging me or getting mad at me. I did not have to be this gangster around her; I never showed Alison that side of myself. I never told her what it was I really did for a living... it wasn't my thing to meet someone and be like; hey I am Greg and I am king of the streets. I push illegal drugs across state lines, and I distribute them up and down the East Coast.

My BMW was year to date, when I first pulled up to her house to take her out to dinner. She believed I was a car dealer until the day she brought my son to see me in prison. I went as far as to purchase a few used car dealerships around the city to fool her. Alison came into my life around the rise of my leadership. Around the time, the FED's started watching my moves. Carlos was on to me; happy and hating at the same time; so while the streets was looking for Pete, I had time to be myself with Alison.

I put both Dee and Alison through college; Dee got the big house, and I brought Alison and nice house. One she would be able to manage on her own if I wasn't around. The house was paid for, the major things was all taken care of; my son's mother had no major worries. Dee had two cars, I brought Alison two cars; neither one of them know they had the same Mercedes-Benz CLK63 AMG series convertible. I took care of my son I had with Alison; I made sure she had a stable home, money, clothes everything she needed to be the mother I wanted to love my child. I was happy when she gave birth to my junior; I knew my child would be safe with her rather than any child I would have had with Dee. The streets didn't know Alison; they knew Dee; even though Dee had a regular job at one point in her life, the streets always associated her with me.

It was not until I got booked is when I got the heart to tell Alison the other side of myself. It was hard telling the other woman that I adored that I was not just a regular hustler; I was the Kingpin. It wasn't until I got booked is when I got the heart to tell the main woman I adored, I had a baby on her; and I wanted to bring him home with me when I got out of jail; to meet her. I knew my words crushed her heart into pieces. When Dee came at me with Kaliyah, I hated Kaliyah so much I let Dee believe she was Alison.

Kaliyah broke the rules I set for her, I paid Kaliyah to stay away from both Dee and myself. When Dee brought Kaliyah to the prison with her and introduced her to Omar. My heart dropped... Dee asked me was it cool for her to bring a friend with her to the visit after Melly stopped fucking with Omar. She never said it was Kaliyah. I pushed Kaliyah out of the picture a long time ago. I thought she was talking about the girl Tisha she used to roll with not Kaliyah!

I could not stand it sitting in there looking at that bitch; there was so much, I wanted to say to her! Including spitting in her face, I decided to take Dee into the bathroom and smash her! I knew we were going to be caught; I knew the guard would come running when he heard me banging on the door. I choked that guard on purpose. Time in the hole was worth not seeing Dee for a while; I did not know how to tell her not to bring that dust-bag with her again, because I knew Kaliyah would have tried to start some shit. That bitch had welfare looking for me for child support.

"What is it about Deandra, that I can't let go of?" Alison asked me things nobody had the ball to ask me. One thing about her, she never bit her tongue when she talked to me. The things she said to me, was the things I needed to hear. Nobody talk to me like she did... her dope-ness was on a different level. I had to ask myself that same shit. However, inside of Dee I can see myself. She hurts like I hurt. She thinks like I think; and she loves hard like I love hard. It's more than the history between us, I always felt like if I saved Dee, I could save myself.

When the street life is all that you know, thinking about what tomorrow will bring to you; is something you do not really want to think about; There are plenty of nights when sleep don't come normal. The higher your position is the more playing opossum becomes normal to you; have you ever taken a nap that felt like the longest nightfall. That ten-minute nap you dosed off for seems like a good eight hours... you suddenly jump up thinking you missed the day... thinking damn! Asking yourself damn how long was I sleep for... then you look at the clock and it has only been ten minutes.

If I can dose off without the streets talking about I have an enemy or someone is coming to take my chicken change from me... I am good. Living in my position and surviving to see another day is okay for me, ten years is years I may not have. Nevertheless, I could not tell Alison something she probably knew but probably did not want to hear. Dee shot me five years to the date; I opened that letter Alison sent me, when she asked me... "Where do I see myself ten years from now?" my mind has not stopped racing since that bullet raced through my leg that Dee shot me with; for the first time I sense myself wishing. Mentally I am praying for forgiveness, asking Allah to have mercy on me; one more day. I just want to answer Alison's questions...

Dee pulled up to the front of Lipstick, to let me out after I sat and watched every player enter. I needed to make a grand entrance. My only orders was to stay put and keep watch of the outside. I knew I could trust her to do that. I knew what it was she was not telling me. Although I did not know the whole story, I knew what I needed to know, so I trusted her to keep watch.

"We are going to start this meeting a little different this morning. I got a call this morning. What I heard, I need it not to be true. A snake is lurking among us! This is the part of the game, that I do not like and I will not tolerate. King Street is home, it is my business... I put in hard work to turn the downfall of one man's empire into the kingdom we all eat from; I will be damn if I will take this disrespect lightly. The person or persons who are responsible for the gunfire that took down my men, my fucking soldiers, will be dealt the code of the streets.

We are going to sort this shit out fast too...I do not plan to do a lot of talking either. One of yall know what happened, the streets don't sleep, but do they talk." I was not on some hello type of shit I had to come straight at them keeping a straight face. The same mentality I had any time some shit went down I did not approve of sailing ship. I already had one snake however; I needed the rest of them.

Chapter 9

King of the Streets

My men and I sat at the round table, whomever that could not fit at the table pulled up seats, in the middle of Lipstick's floor. The same spot where the ballers used to throw dollars at the strippers. Lipstick became my meetinghouse ever since the cops ran up in there and locked up all the clubs most valuable patrons. The Rathouse they nicknamed it; I felt bad so I brought Cory another place downtown. My plans was to turn this jawn into a restaurant or something. Without telling a soul, I made a call to my sharp shooters, when Dee went into the diner to grab us something to eat. I waited in the car. Nobody knew I had the building surrounded.

Mr. Stilks 5th streets Captain, sat next to Donny 7th street Captain, the only time you saw north sit next to south is, when they sat in front of me. Donny splattered blood on Mr. Stilks cousin that feud between them was personal. Uptown Willie sat elbow to elbow to Germantown Craig. Southwest Charlie sat next to me although I am Uptown my most profitable hustler got my honor. Omar was on the other side of me. West Philly Showtime dusty ass sat far on the left next to Jersey George, and New York's Albert. Maryland's Randy and DC's Spencer concluded the list of the round table.

The mental notes started fifth teen minutes past noon, none of anything we talked about; was allowed to be written on paper. I rather for my players to forget, what had been said then to leave a paper trail. We did not keep the same numbers; we kept separate phones for different people. Each Captain had a code to use when they called me direct, no text messages, beepers we still had them. No one was allowed to call a Top Players phone more than two times a week from the same number. The trap phones numbers was changed on payday.

The only players that was allowed to make runs to personal callers was the Lower Ends. Top Players were not allowed to answer to those calls, because we never knew when someone was going to try to set us up. Besides that, a Top Players bail would cost higher than a Lower End. I was a paranoid so I ran my business on pins and needles. However this meeting was different, I took my notes with my pistol. I had a bad feeling, I did not want to tell Dee what I knew; I did not want to get baby girls panties in a bunch. I kept my feelings to myself. As the Captains discussed the he said she said shit; I sat quiet watching. I already knew who shot the block up, but what I needed to know is who has behind my reasons.

As the ringleader, of the gang it was only right for me to let my right-hand be speaker of the house. I on the other hand, after I said what I said, was waiting for anyone to start talking different, so I just paid attention. Omar let me down; he was running that meeting like a fucking kindergarten cop! Asking questions and making statements as if this was some playhouse shit. I knew what time I was on as far as getting to the bottom of this nonsense. My patience were short, the players was starting to look at me like what the fuck... Omar was on some other stuff.

"Do we have beef I don't know about?" Said the Kindergarten cop...

"Where were you when the block got shot?" Fucking Kindergarten Cop...

"Who is responsible, for the shooting?" Fucking Kindergarten Cop...

"What is your ambition in this game?" Really... fucking Kindergarten Cop...

"What kind of car do you drive?" What... fucking Kindergarten Cop...

"Where do you live?" I zoned out listening to that fucking Kindergarten Cop...

Not Omar, my main man. If it were not for Omar, I would not be the King of the streets. His brother was my connection to the dope; he could not be me because I was heir to the throne. Carlos did not fight me when I took the streets from him.

When he found out, I was Pete he dabbed me pound, and welcomed me to his spot. He was in the mist of doing something bigger. His status in politics was his focus. Then from out of nowhere, Mr. Stilks steps out of position and interrupts Omar... I was glad somebody else stopped the bullshit. I was short-tempered trying to hold on... I was seconds from just shooting and blowing the whistle for my sharp shooters to start shooting nigga's; all I heard was...

"Gee listen man no disrespect to you; but I am not the feeling this interrogation shit. Omar I don't know what tip you are on... call it disrespect, I don't care at this point... I don't fuck with you anyway prick... you lost your touch to the streets; I am going to keep this shit one hundred... when yall two was down I was the backbone to this ship. So let's be honest, just be quiet and listen Mister Omar! We are beyond this chitter chatter. Man King Street been on the verge of a take down. We all know that, but the question is who put it on the verge? Who let these goons think they are tough like that? Last time I checked we ran this city.

All honesty you have to move ship... Gee, you cannot use King Street anymore! That block is going to get too hot! I think for the best interest of your empire, that you don't do business with some of these ungrateful nigga's... Fuck a rat... I smell a snake. Fuck a position and fuck who is listening or who is offended.

I am a firm believer of the street code. I used to get my dope from Carlos, I know how this game twist and turn.

I can speak for my men and myself... my team Gucci... We do not have nothing to do with last night, nor what has been happening. However, since you have been loyal to us Gee, selling me the best dope, never cheating me. Never crossing me. Never steering me wrong, or having me believe different. I have mad respect for you Gee. Therefore, here is my proposition... I have ears to the streets out there right now, and my goons are ready to pop anybody that is out of order no questions asked. I got your back Gee for real man. Just say the word and my men will cock and reload." Mr. Stilks was the coolest old head I knew. I never had a problem with him, so I just nodded to him in agreements... the thing about Stilks was I knew I could trust him. However, Omar did not like it at all.

"It wasn't your turn Stilks, you know the fucking rule speak when you are spoken too... pay the table five- hundred for your long winded speech... and who the fuck you think you are talking direct to me? What the fuck is wrong with you? You got beef with Mister Omar. Talking this gangster shit out of your mouth, fuck what you did when I wasn't here... I'm here now got a problem with that Mr. Stilks?" Mister Omar must have lost his marbles. I liked Mr. Stilks, he taught me some of the, thrillist shit I know. He warned me about Omar when I was in jail, telling me to watch him. Nevertheless, I felt like Omar gave me no reason to feel like that; damn I had to interfere.

"Thank you Stilks, I really appreciate your words because I knew they are facts; some of yall Captain's need to take notes. Stilks is a thorough breed, pick yall faces up yall look disordered. Moving forward, before Stilks and Omar blow this meeting off course. There is no need for yall two to go back and forth, come on right-hand... you and I both know this is some bullshit; and you and I both know the street code is changing.

Stilks is right; you, you, you, you and all of you... know something, yall know King Street was my official warning that I have a Snake afloat. I personally lost three men last night; I have two in critical. I need names; I came to yall because yall are the ones who are in charge of the hoppers. Something this major needs to be addressed by the head players. Because King Street belongs to me, so that means someone is after me! Either its one of yall or one of yall hoppers stepping up to the throne.

My distribution house is not to be fucked with; I like to know whom I have beef with because I want to sleep tonight. I am not ready to give up my spot, just like the president, he can't leave the office being the man without starting or ending the turn of a war." Cocky Greg is what they called me behind my back. I never gave a fuck about how many people liked me, as long as they respected me, we was cool.

"Greg, chill I got this... Stilks ain't nobody to be calling shots, but what he need to do is shut the fuck up; you don't know shit Stilks. Your Gucci players G's are P's straight pussy... kitten shit, how many major moves did yall fuck up this quarter alone? Shit if I didn't know better sounds like you are the Snake. Suck my snake, since you like to be a dick jockey." Omar commented. That shit was funny, but I wasn't laughing.

"Chill, you don't got shit... I am ashamed of how this meeting is going. Therefore, I need the streets to know how mad I am... call it what you want... but King Street as I repeat is my house. I built that shit... it is me they are after! So since nobody want to talk on this open floor... nobody... going once... nobody...that was twice. Fuck, you for saying fuck me. I hope you and your men have enough, it is going to be a cold summer. Everybody is cut off!

Fuck all yall, if you think you are getting dope from me... you better off going to the unemployment line to find you a regular nine-to-five. I am done doing business with you. I am King of the streets, thinking about coming after my chicken scraps, be prepared to get dealt with; try to outsource to someone else watch me cock and reload. Try me in here if you want too... get out my house!" then I singled for my sharp shooters to blow cover; none of the Captains where strapped I had them searched at the door.

"Hold up Gee, not cool this could be the start of a turf war, we don't need that baby boy..." Showtime replied...

"I don't care bust the move my men right there..." I replied pointing to my sharp shooters.

"Naw man, not with you but how I am going to tell my men I can't get the work anymore you are the only one with it man..." Maryland's Randy stated...

"So, what do I care they don't run for me..."

"Gee, come on man how long have we been doing business man..." Mr. Stilks I liked him...

"Look Stilks, respect is due to a dog I will be damn if I sit here quiet acting all jolly like I don't know snakes is lurking; I feel you of all people. This shit is personal..." I dismissed all of the Captains from the building; the only person left was Omar and me, one of my sharp shooter's researched us both as we enter into what used to be the VIP room. My shooter stood outside.

"Damn Omar I thought we was better than that... that meeting was some bullshit man what's wrong you good? Talk to me..." Then as he started to talk, his jibber jabber... I zoned out...

Mister Omar my right-hand man, I learned in prison that I had to play him close. Yeah he was in there dookie whipping with the faggots. My cellmate put me on to him, but I just looked at it as if it was none of my business. I was in there holding my own trying to keep my name up in the streets outside of the jail walls. For the simple fact, I didn't want to come home to no bullshit. I had a bad bitch on my team; I was thinking how I could lose. Only a few players knew I was locked up: Omar, Melly, Dee, Alison, Kaliyah, my mother and my brother Cory; oh and Mister Stilks... but Carlos was the one who cut my time short.

Damn this Omar shit was killing me; my mother was the first woman to break my heart. I did not think it could get any worst then that. If someone had told me years ago, the fall of my empire would be because of the fall of me, for falling in love with a bad bitch; I do not know if I would had still been out there trying to save Dee. I never understood why Carlos made the moves he did as far as keeping family on the down side of his street life affairs. Yeah Vanessa was down to make moves with him... but the most of what Vanessa did was the family shit. She kept the kids from going into the child welfare system.

Vanessa's doings limited a lot of shit; Carlos needed her more than that, because Vanessa was the money Carlos needed. That cop paycheck of his was petty cash. That chump change did nothing for him but give him a political status... it was the drug money that gave him the power. It was his security to play in the streets, noble cop or corrupted cop... he was untouchable. No shooter out there wanted to go down for killing a cop; the city would take his side and take your head. Naw the street niggas loved their drugs...we left shit like that for regular broke Nigga's!

Therefore, we baptized Carlos situation different... shit he was the one who started this shit... he opened the docks to bring in ship. As for me, I was just Gee the corner rocker, the only one that had the balls to step up and take the crown of the Kingpin. Carlos was too busy working on his political position running for Police Chief, he could not stop me. He needed to disconnect his self for a minute anyway, because the streets was getting too searing. It was almost like he gave it to me... when he found out I was Pete he dabbed me pound, I never had beef with him. In fact, he schooled me to the top. I'm guessing he figured, without Melly and without me; he would be penniless and pathetic with enemies.

I promised him that one day we would be able to come to the table and break bread. It was only right he used to feed me; and not to mention he never came after me after we hit up his distribution house. Carlos was like a father to me, he knew the code of the streets, and I guess, he rather for it to be blood and not Sylvester. I was twenty-three when I found out Carlos was my dad. I never told Dee we were kissing cousins. Well come to find out Carlos was married into the Jameson family, him and Antonio was not even blood brothers; Carlos was Antonio's Sr. other wife son. When she died, Antonio Sr. raised Carlos as his own.

I loved Melly, when I got the news about my relations I just kept that shit to myself. It was just too much... Melly never knew my mother was Carlos secrete lover; that crazy love triangle hit close to home Dee's brother, Shaun is my blood brother. Damn I don't think Dee know just how much I love her too. My bitch held me down, then put me out for dead. She was my ride or die; Dee always showed me love, she capitalized my G. I brought out the woman in her and she brought out the man in me, or so she tried... I always showed her the big ass boy... that is what she calls me. If I died that day or the next, no matter how I was to go out. I knew in my heart millions was going to show up at my funeral; just to make sure I was dead. Therefore, my patience was starting to tick... I tuned back in...

"Omar let me ask you something my man... why Dee?" I said getting straight to the point...

"What do you mean?"

"You fucked her didn't you?"

"What are you talking about man?"

"You fucked Dee... you got beef with me I don't know about?"

"What..."

"I thought I would have gotten the call from you, about the shooting on King Street. However, Mr. Stilks was calling to inform me that my right-hand was out to get me. I don't owe you a mother fucking thing Coot, you want me... here I am... what's up nigga?"

"You don't deserve to be the King of the streets, look at you... do you hear yourself pussy talking to Omar like Omar is a bitch. It's your bitch that you need to check!"

"My bitch... what do she have to do with this besides pussy spitting on your balls?"

"Thomas is after you, you fucked his bitch... he knows... He also knows your bitch stole his money and gave my contracts to you... you was going to out me? Haven't I given you enough? You want Omar's chicken change too. I can't have no money; but you are not going to answer that are you? Because you are too busy trying to figure out if I fucked your bitch! I am not the only one who fucked your bitch... Sylvester fucked your bitch but I bet you knew that; oh and if you think about doing shit about what I just said... do yourself a favor and don't.

See you was my man but how can I say that you are my man when all do is steal and tell. You told on the El Pablo's, after you and Melly took their money from their cash house. You could have given up... but no your greed is unbelievable man. I am talking millions yall stole. But you know with stolen millions came humble million years, of enemies following. I never knew Dee was the one who set up Lipstick that night, yeah your brother's club. Your bitch is playing you pussy.

Yeah we got beef now; because I didn't believe it until I noticed my money is missing. You closed the accounts on me. Not to mention you sitting here fraudin with this right-hand man shit. Greg you, been pushed me out... Why I never knew you lived in Alpine? You cannot be the Kingpin in any streets because you are a rat Gee. Jahgie is not feeling you man, how do you and Melly make plots with the Choppers then burn them. If I would have known what type of snake, I befriended I would have never done business with you or Keliney. The two of yall are toxic...you played me fam... I am done, being your right hand Greg. So hand over the money or I give the orders to end the ransom and alert the search team.

No body have to know about this little talk it's between you and me; I did not shoot up your house, and I don't have Thomas or the kid; if that's what you are going to ask me next. However, I do know who has them and, and where they are, I know where the kid is being held. Therefore, if you want my information, you give me the contract payments, which was ten million over five years; I will accept the buyout because I know the Choppers drew blood on King Street. I feel like that was part my fault; I told them Pete was you. So with the contracts... give me what you owe the Choppers and I will put everything back in order. Oh and as for my brother he will be contacting you after this meeting to let your know the deal is off. Oh and Maine Street... it's done, I sold it to the Choppers bitch..."

"Just like that, wow... I never been a rat, yeah I helped Melly and when we partook on that transaction, we knew we became not only humble millionaires; but named humble millionaires because we took what wasn't going to be given to us. It was ours we worked for it in reality. Therefore, before you judge something you know nothing about on information you got from rats don't take it upon yourself to address me about it.

What you forgot you took the money too? Or did the dick up your ass make you forget? So if I am a thief... so are you Poppy! I bet if you wasn't such a dick thirsty follower you would have known what really went down in the cash house. Naw, you are too busy sucking on Choppers dicks, to realize they are using you! But what gives you think I am a bitch... We also know with those humble millions, we would become humble million years. Do you know what that mean faggot?" I replied...

"Faggot, funny slim... but I'm not playing and my offer is not going to stand on the table for long... you are done slim. Me and my brother is taking over the streets, see we always looked down on the Choppers, I guess that's what rivals do to each other. However, my Chopper beef was never personal, to my understanding they was your problem player. I enjoy working with the Choppers, they are smart... maybe they will give you a job in your own hood... bitch... How is Dee doing? Tell her the Choppers got her family and Omar said his daughter is pretty." Omar...Omar... I thought...

"So you are saying if I take you on this offer you will end this? Okay they want the streets or the docks I am confused, you are saying money, so is it just chicken change or is it more that you are not telling me while we are still cool..."

"Look here, I will take the out; I am saying you can buy me out since you are pushing me out anyway, and I will disappear without a fight; one hundred million large. I know you have it; we run a billion dollar organization. What I am asking for is nothing. The Choppers want all, but I am sure the fifty large chicken change will call them off... shit this whole thing could have been over if this wasn't your first time showing your face for minute. You want to be all Hollywood on the same players that should have popped you years ago. You balling and they are still hungry thinking you are the same Uptown Kingpin. Before they met me they was still looking for Pete." Wow I thought...damn...

"Wow, so you are the snake... well I am not a rat... so listen I knew when I became a humble millionaire... that I was officially a humble million year. A millionaire with a million enemies following me; never would I have thought Omar would be one of the million. You know I am not surprised; it comes with the territory of being King of the Streets. I earned my position and we both know that faggot. Funny you didn't know I know you are a dookie whipper... hun? Well I am far from a bitch, therefore, since I am not dick thirsty... faggot fuck you... if you want me I am right here." I said folding my arms for him to try me...

"Cool, I should have fucked you in the ass, pussy... twenty-four hours pay the ransom. I'll handle my portion the dock drop is mine! Come after me and I will shoot you. Sleep on that partner; you are done... oh and something else... Cory your mother's son fucked your bitch too! So to answer your question yeah I fucked your bitch, and it was good too, Omar see why Greg go hard for his bitch Dee!"

Then as he stood up to walk out of the room, I called him and when he turned around; I pulled the gun I had tucked in my drawls my shooter knew I had, and I shot Omar in his nuts, so that he could feel my agony. Thomas could fuck my bitch, because he wasn't my homie. I lost my right-hand man that day; I shot him seven times, six times directly in the head.

Thomas, damn I would give it to him he is a smart man. Although, this was not the way you want to meet the Kingpin; I never met him in person I only saw his picture. I didn't even know how much of this drama Dee and I was into he knew. I knew he knew about me because Dee was still living with me when she left me for him. I could have been petty a long time ago, but I knew my relationship with Dee, was not going to get no better it was best we parted ways...damn she played me...

Chapter 10

Dusty Bitch

I walked out of Lipstick feeing like shit, with my hand on fire; ready to protect my name, by all means necessary. I got back into the car on the passenger side with Dee who was still sitting in the driver's seat. My Shooter let me know beforehand, that is was cool. I now had another man riding with me; he was sitting in line to follow me to my next move. I never liked mind games, but I wanted to live. I wanted to see my son again. The grave wasn't the place I wanted him to see me... some don't want to see jail again, once they have been released, however if jail was going to be the place my son would have to come visit me then so be it; I wasn't going to die because of a dusty-bitch.

"You good baby girl?" I asked her...

"Are you okay? I feel like something is up... I didn't see Omar come out. I counted everyone even ah few extras I didn't see go in, but I didn't see Omar."

"He left out back." I replied...

"But his car is right over there, where did he go?"

"In that black truck right there... he good, we cool. Come on switch seats with me I am driving..." I got out and walked around the car I let Dee slide over; She looked at me crazy, when I pushed the door lock, and peeled off in a fast pace. "We never got the chance to finish our conversation. Tell me the truth as you know it; is Journey mine?" I asked her...

"Where did that come from?"

"The other day up on the hill, Kathy interrupted us... I was about to ask you that before she came up and cut me off."

"Funny you ask, I was starting to question that, she don't look nothing like my husband." Damn Dee I thought to myself...

"That don't mean nothing, I see a lot of her grandmother in her..."

"You think she looks like Melody?"

"Yeah I see the resemblance..."

"You never told me what the paternity test results were... You came all the way out to Cali just to swab my mouth..."

"I never got them back, I called but they told me the results was mailed out and they couldn't give me the results over the phone..."

"Question, when were you going to tell me you smashed my man and you smashed my brother?" The look on her face was priceless, I do not know who baby girl thought she was about to play. "You don't have nothing to say hun?"

"What do my pussy have to do with what is going on Greg, I never fucked the homie's, and you fucked my homie..."

"Deandra, you haven't change a bit... Same scheming, mean, lost, dusty Bitch... I thought we were better than this. We did a lot for each other, you are alive because of me and the feeling is mutual. I fucked up and I owned up to it and I can admit that; I smashed the homie yeah; now I am stuck with my mistake for life... but what makes my mistake different is my mistake ain't going to kill you. You fucked up Dee big time; what you thought I was not going to find out? You would have been better off sticking me up yourself mask off.

I have been right here next to you the whole time. I have so much shit going on already and now you want parts in it; your set up failed I know Bitch... I know... so stop looking at me stupid and talk to me bitch, I am trying to be nice... and if you think about touching that door... bitch I will murk you on everything I love..."

"Just shoot me Greg, I don't care anymore... I am sorry I don't know what you are talking about;

all I did was try to help you... I am not the one after you..."

"That's it...you think this shit is a game... you lied on me, then you took the information I gave you...and you used it against the wrong people! You a rat that is why you ran to Africa...you used me, I confided in you and you played me. Now you got your husband out here looking for me. You stole from him, you lied on me... you stole from me... now you are sitting here lying to me. What contract did I take from you? What money did I steal from Omar? You made it seem like I was in on taking Carlos and them down; is that why you keep questioning my association with Melly. Dee you got me in the middle of some bullshit... I cannot do this this shit with you anymore."

"Damn..." was all she said shaking her head... I put my gun to her head, my trigger finger was telling me to shoot her... but my heart told me not too...

"Go head pull it, I am sorry for what I did... I can't take back nothing what's done is done. Pull it or give it to me and I will pull it..."

"You a bad bitch, you think I am going to let you off the hook that easy... the only reason why Omar went out in a body bag was because he disrespected me; I am sensitive when it comes to my feelings... your ass got nigga's thinking I am some kind of bitch..."

"Would you believe me if I told you the truth?" this Bitch been around me too long I thought to myself, her chill tone of voice made me feel like I was talking to myself.

"You don't get it… you are going to help me out of this and you want to know how? I know who has Journey, but the tables have turned… either you can work with me to get these goons off us or I do to you what you have done to me; Dee you are going to be my bait."

"Where is she?" She cried out…I wonder if those where real tears…

"Bait or trade you pick…" I said returning the same chill tone of voice I knew she hated. Yet she used on me.

"Greg please can I tell you the truth please… please I want my daughter, I never wanted to hurt you; I never intended for this to blow up like this… Greg slow down please …." The tears started to fall … they touched me… fuck I almost shot her…

"I am telling you now if you plan on lying to me save it! Take it to your grave and just hope I don't dump your body in the river."

"Greg, I am sorry for not telling you the truth, I am sorry for coming at you the way that I did! I did not tell anyone that you told me what Carlos and them was into; I put things into my own words with the information Taylor gave me about Antonio and Mona. I never testified on Carlos, I never testified on Melly; I went to her trial for support not to convict her. Yes, I knew the FED's was going to make that bust that night at Lipstick; I could not tell you, Greg I wanted to so bad but I knew you would not approve of it. I did not want you to be caught in the middle of things... You said it was none of my business, but I had everything to do with it! Mona abused me and you know it, Antonio raped Taylor; Mona drugged my brother, she abused him; there was nights we did not eat.

Yes, I wanted retaliation; my revenge had nothing to do with your empire or theirs. Do you know what it feels like not to know nothing about yourself do you know what it feels like to be me? I never put you out there, I would never put you out there, and what contracts did I give you what are you talking about?"

"That wasn't cool you right I would not approve of you ratting... what you think I don't hurt? I have feelings too I am human. Just because I can pull a trigger and pop somebody, do not mean that I like it... in theses streets... its kill or be killed. Omar blamed you he said my bitch stole contracts from her husband and put my name on them... So where is Thomas so I can clear my name with him...?"

"What contracts are you talking about, Thomas don't have nothing to do with this... Omar is lying..."

"Well mister Omar is dead so who is it and why are you not talking fast enough, because I have an idea but before I react I want to make sure what I know match what is true. Because I was waiting for this day to come a lot of shit over some time just wasn't adding up..."

"I met up with Omar by accident; I was on vacation in St, Thomas with my husband and I ran into Omar. I introduced him to Thomas and the two hit it off; I did not tell Thomas how I knew Omar or that he knew you... I told Omar about Thomas's hotel business and the ones he owns here in America. Thomas was opening a new Hotel in Miami; Omar pulled him to the table and them two signed contracts. I did not know Omar had traded teams; he pulled me to the side at the grand opening of Thomas's hotel resort.   He wanted me to introduce Sal to Thomas because Sal was his business partner with trafficking the laborers.

I told Omar no, I explained that I did not trust Sal, but Omar went behind my back and did it anyway. When I found out what was going on I told Thomas to void the contracts. Thomas ended up using another company some Russians. I did not hear from Omar for a while. Kathy called me to do her a favor, she wrote to the governor to have Melly's appeal approved. She offered me money and it was enough money to help get me away from Thomas without using his money. She asked me to do a story on how I exposed the Jameson's brothers, and why I took the plea not to take the stand. Taylor was the one who ran to the media... I was not going to say what she had said; I was only focused on what Mona had done to me. I was desperate Greg."

"What do any of that have to do with me?" I said...my nerves was ticking...

"Omar called me before I landed at the airport from out of nowhere... he told me that he wanted to meet up and like a fool I went to meet him. He told me you were looking for me, and you wasn't happy, because you heard about us sleeping together and you was having a bitch fit. He went on to tell me that you was planning to do something crazy to get me back. I didn't pay him any mind because I knew I had just spoken to you. Therefore, I just went on about my business and that was that... I didn't respond to him because I didn't even know how he knew I was even in New York.

Omar followed me to Grand Central Station when I was coming to meet you; and that is why I rerouted you. I came to you with the paternity bull because I needed Omar to see me meeting with you. I told him that you were living out there, that is why I asked you not to get off the train and to take a flight out of Atlanta to go to Cali. I knew Omar never knew where you lived in Jersey. It had nothing to do with Thomas finding out that we were still friends.

When I came to Cali to meet you. I never wanted to hurt you... I did not let Omar wire me either; I told him that I was going to have sex with you. He was planning to take you out... that is why I closed the accounts you and him shared that was in my name. I paternity tested you because I changed Journey's birth certificate and put your name on it...I made a Will, my wishes was for you to take care of Journey, I left yall everything. The money he wants is in my daughter's name. Thomas do not have anything to do with it... I have your money I never crossed you. I couldn't tell you then because I did have an affair with Omar and he was going to show my husband the tape he secretly recorded of us without my knowledge. Thomas beats me, but without Thomas, I have nothing. My marriage is not perfect it hurts...He does not know the Russians are really me. I was planning to leave him... He is not the person I married.

They came after me because they knew I was the only one who could get close to you. Sal was the one who put Thomas on the phone... I know it; he is the only one who calls me pretty face. He wants your spot, Omar was doing business with him, and it has to be Sal... I overheard Omar talking about making big moves that he did not need your permission... Omar used me..." She was telling me the truth... then again it could have been a lie... I don't know about Thomas beating on her but some of what she said was the truth...

"Here call that number back... I am gonna do the talking..." I believed her Omar had been acting funny for a while. Mister Stilks told me he seen O talking to Sal when he came to King Street to pick up his work. Sal was a rat and a thief all the soldiers that worked under me knew not to trust him...he was the reason why Melly could not come back to the crew.

Damn Omar put me out there he told Sal that I was Pete. Pete was more than just being the Kingpin; Mr. Stilks Had the most workers in the city working under him, he could have been the Kingpin; but I owned the Docks I brought the work in; my men and I pushed it across state-lines. Push everything, take everything, was Pete; power, earnings, takeover, everything was Pete. All of Stilks workers worked under me... the East Coast Kingpins all got their work from me Pete the King of the streets. I was the man that knew the man but that man was me and Omar... but Omar could not own the streets, because I inherited them. That rat Sal wanted my empire; he wants my chicken change... I declared war... using Dee as my bait.

Chapter 11

Reloaded

I stripped Dee of all weapons in the back seat of the car... as she cried out for me to stop hitting her. I had never put my hands on her the way that I gave it to her. The bitch kicked me when I pulled her from out of the car. My love for her was deep; but slowly it was fading away. I just could not believe my heart would set me up! Of all the people that wanted to save her, she traded on me. I could not grasp it around my mind that someone I loved would do what she had done to me. I was not a woman beater... I grow up watching men smack on the women around me; that was not my style. I had to show her my affection was real; I had to show her that I was hurt. I had to show her my worth. Then I took pictures of her, the only proof I made a printed note of and sent it to the snakes.

My informant told me that Thomas was hesitant about Dee's whereabouts, thank God, somebody really had my back; and that was the last person I would think to have it, crazy but true. Dee put me at war on both sides of the streets. I had gangsters coming looking for me to take my empire from me... I had my old bitch husband looking for me thinking I stole from him and fucked his bitch. Before Cincinnati, I never had an affair with Dee. When I said I was done with her I was done with her. We kept in contact for friendship, nothing more than checking on each other. After all, she still had money of mine in her name.

Never did I stop loving her, I just could not love her the same. I wished I had watched her closer... crazy someone else was watching what I should have been paying attention too. Busted lip, bloody nose, and a naked body in the back seat of a car... Worked wonders for the pictures. Proof I had Dee held for ransoms. Sylvester; wanted my empire, finally he found out Pete was me; the code of the streets say a rat cannot be a kingpin; but I wasn't a rat I was King of the Streets. Sal's rise to the ringleader of the Chester Choppers only went down because Antonio was weak.

He had the thirsty hoes thinking he was Mack Daddy; Sal was a hopper whose boss gave him too much power to call shots. Only the broke base-heads wanted the lightweight he sold. What my Captains purchased from me was street gold... much more powerful than any thirty-six Sal's Jamaicans brought into the States. Sal and his team may have been water whipping thirty-six's on a regular, twenty's and tens was the most they could profit off a bag. My men counted on average a million a week and that was just during the end of a month. Thirty-six that is a kilo; my personal players that worked straight out of my trap house flipped thirty-six's a person a shift during the first through the fifth-teen of the month...

Sal wants my chicken change, these pictures will bring him to it; a lot of players had to learn the hard way not to judge me by my looks. Cocky because I was about that life, one cannot be the King of the dope yet scared to shoot. Melly was the finest to ever do it; I knew she was hurt when she found out I had to knock off her brother who was supposed to be dead. Dee was more like her mother than what she wanted to believe; Melly never told me Jeff was Jasper. The same Jay that helped Antonio kidnap her kids back in the days. She never came at the Jameson's brothers because she wanted them to go down for offing him.

Omar sent him to come look for me; Jeff had been living like a woman. Main reason why nobody could find him, Melly knew about him. Just as I helped to hide her, she and Omar helped to hide him... I had been using Plover Street for personal use for the longest, it was the place Melly, Omar and I would go, and pack from time to time whenever they was in town from New York. Melly and I had buried some money in there, five-hundred large; we figured if one of us were to get bail, the bail would have been at least ten percent of a million, which is one hundred thousand, we buried a total half of the million in the floorboard under the carpet. The rest was our fugitive capitol.

The damage Omar did with telling his brother not to do business with me was vicious. He not only had the Choppers looking for me but the Hispanics where out to get me. This was Mr. Stilks chance to prove to me that he was a trusted rider. The Hispanics was strong in North Philly. I was aware of Omar's brother setting up shop in house up there. He was working with Omar to take over the East Coast streets with the help of the Choppers. My shooter I kept on hand was Carlos; he was home from jail on an appeal and wanted his turn with the rat Sal, who was in position to testify against him in court. The evidence that once convicted him was not enough to hold him down on the murder charges. Sal snitched that's why him and a few other Choppers got out of jail early.

Dee was telling the truth, but she wasn't telling me the whole truth. The only reason why she wanted to get away from Thomas was, because she needed to disappear without Thomas following her. No matter what anyone said about Carlos, he was an amazing cop, bad cop yeah... but the work he did was genius. When we got over our awkward tensions, he reasonably became my backbone; Mr. Stilks always told me not to trust Omar; but I wasn't sure if I could trust someone who always told me not to trust someone. Therefore, Mr. Stilks was the perfect person to induct as my right-hand. Carlos didn't need to know all of my moves, although we was cool; I didn't feel certain that I should trust him.

I offered Stilks the dock drop, which my other sharp shooters guarded. It was worth 3.5 million in street value. On one note, he took on Bridge Street. I was a one-man army, I was desperate I needed help. I couldn't trust Dee in the same percentage I couldn't trust Carlos. I had to reload the game plan. After Dee called the number back, Sal gave us twenty-four hours to meet him on Maine Street for the trade. Maine Street was already on my stop list that is where the drugs went to be organized after they came off the docks. That was Pete house not King Street.

King Street was my house the streets knew about. I hit King Street because I needed a reason to call my Captain's to the table; and it was the only way that I was going to be able to get Omar to show his face to me... he fell for it because he was too busy plotting on mugging Maine Street. I had gotten word that Maine Street had been robbed an hour after, I called the meeting for the Captains, to talk about King Street.

The players I shot favored Omar they was the team he brought to the table. If I had not called him, into the VIP room Omar was going to keep pleading the fifth and pretending he was not in on the plot. Going to the police was just not an option for me; who was going to care about a drug dealer being ran out of his power by other drug dealers. Therefore, after I reloaded the game plan I restarted my mental notes, checking off the humble million years of my enemies... in rout with a few of my friendemies.

Chapter 12

Money Power Respect:

Mr. Stilks the Man of the Hour

"**G**reg, you have my word, like I said in the meeting my men are on it. However, how can you assure me that this shit won't come back to me or that you are not double-crossing? You cut me and my men off the supply..."

"Stilks I know what I did man... you and I both know you are the only Captain in the hood that I can trust with this job. Look, I am Pete, King Street is not the only merchandise that I run, Pete is not my boss, and he is not someone I work for... he is me... so listen I have 3.5 million dollars' worth of supply down on the docks. My men are down there right now keeping watch. All of it can be yours if you do me one favor." Greg replied over the phone. Damn I thought to myself this young nigga had me fooled. Greg never revealed to anyone that he was Pete himself. The Captains just thought him and Omar was the messengers... if Greg was really Pete... damn he fooled me... Damn I didn't know what to believe...

"3.5 million, for one favor?" I questioned...

"One favor that's it..." Damn that sounded good but I wasn't impressed.

"What is the favor?"

"I found out who is after me, if they get me... you and your men and everyone else don't get the supply yall need and want. You was right I couldn't trust Omar. He sold me out to the Choppers..."

"The Choppers want you?" I wasn't surprised but I knew I would need more than some drugs for a payment.

"They want to take everything the docks the distribution house everything..." I could tell by the tone of his voice that he was sincere, not to mention we never talked this long over the phone before...

"I am going to have to move my family on this, the Choppers fight dirty..."

"Look I will handle the Choppers; I have something they want right now that will hold them off, and its worth more then what they can take from me."

"You do know that the Choppers cannot be trusted, what whatever gold you have it better be more than 24karts... so what is it you need from me that you are willing to give me 3.5million in supply for free?"

"On top of the supply, I have fifty million cash with no strings attached all for you..."

"Damn Gee, it must be serious 3.5 and 50 cash no strings attached what I have to do man sign me up..." I was thinking shit with that amount of income and that amount of supply shit I could make that move and a few others moves of my own. Take down the Hispanics on Bridge Street...I was familiar with the runners up there, they gave my men competition; I was already looking for a way to bust a move on them. Gee was my man, I respected him 100percent; his power was strong before he showed me his fragile side. Now I am no snake, I am a hustler and when hustlers see opportunity, they don't sit on it; however they act on it.

My family knew what I was into, and they knew whenever I said pack up and move into hiding they had to be ready to go. I had everyone counted for except for my wife Natalie and my daughter Natalia. I had my mother, sisters and their kids, my brothers and their kids and wives... I had my other baby mom and our four kids. I loaded everyone up in two vans; I went to the school and I picked up my sons, hoping to run into Natalie, but she wasn't there. I must have called her phone over ten-times... no answer...

The clock with Greg was ticking, but I need my woman and my daughter. Therefore, after I got the rest of my family onto the road heading down south, I stayed behind to follow my orders and wait for Natalie to call me back. I called seven of my most trusted soldiers to run down Bridge Street with me. For us it was a turf war; but for me it was my bounty. My men and I fired-bombed the four homes, all belonging to Omar's people.

Omar's brother Pablo I handled personally, when he stepped on the scene, he told me to my face he was taking my streets if I didn't move. My beef with him was personal.

Greg was a man of his word, fifty in cash and a mountain of drugs. No strings attached... then as the two, of us shook hands I could see Carlos watching from a car that was parked behind mine! I did not know what those two were up too... I thought Carlos was in jail, "what the fuck" I thought to myself.

"Is that, who I think it is back there Gee, is there something you want to tell me?" I questioned...

"Thank you, Mr. Stilks you did a fine job today..." Damn my heart started racing...

"Gee don't play with me man, that's Carlos..." My first thought was why me...

"Yeah, he is cool what do double the cash price mean... are you willing to double up or are you done?" I had a feeling one favor meant a dollar for each dollar he paid me. You cannot become a millionaire in the hood, without gaining a humble million years of enemies following you... or a million years of favors coming on behalf of you; so that you can pay your million-dollar commission back to the hood. Even with all the money in the world, this drug life is hard to leave alone and even harder to live free and happy. More money equals more problems... is the realest shit ever. Whoever made that quote up must have been a gangster... However, I knew I could not skip town without my wife and my daughter who was still uncounted for...

"What is it man you only said one..." I replied...

"Help me find whoever loves Jahgie..."

"Oh you want Estelle?"

"I want his attention..."

"His attention is worth my double?"

"Yeah, your double price is worth the price he put on my head, it's only fair that I give him a taste of his own medicine."

"What do Carlos have to do with it? Didn't you take the streets from him?"

"Naw I inherited the streets from him..."

"Inherited?"

"You are asking too many questions Stilks either you taking or you are walking... I don't have a story to entertain you with..." Greg's cocky demeanor was hard to pre-judge, I really could not tell if he was weak as I thought in the beginning or was his slender body frame, really the powerful King of the Streets he mimicked his self to be. I never had no problems with him, and this was the first time he ever really showed this side of him to me. I mean I heard shit about him being coo-coo for coco puffs, likewise I do not think he ever saw the other side of me. Naw yes, he did, I thought to myself damn... the King of the Streets was a smart nigga ... Damn...

"You right, let's go I'm on it…" Gee was a man of his word and I knew I could trust him to pay me any amount he quoted to me; I was however, skeptical on how many more favors he was going to drag me into.

Shit he saw right through my greedy ass! I only said yes because I already knew I was leaving after I found my wife, and on some real stuff… if I didn't talk to her after this bid… I was leaving her ass. My feelings was getting excited! I got into Greg's car as the two of us drove to Chester with Carlos following behind; also, another car was behind Carlos, which I could see from the side mirror that was following along in the side lane. I got a good glance at the driver; it was one of the Uptown players, so I figured he must have called his boys for back up.

Which was cool, I was only thinking of myself at that moment. Shit, I had a handful of my men down on the docks collecting my money, power and respect. Stilks was coming back to be a boss somewhere else… I laughed to myself saying shit Philly is too hot for Mr. Stilks… I was thinking Greg could have his dirty streets back… and busted hoes. While he drove, I just sat quiet, he was mute and so was I … when he asked where to go I just pointed my finger.

Chapter 13

Humble Million Years
Back with Greg

Riding in the car with Mr. Stilks, I could tell he wasn't feeling the moment; something was up, I felt like he was making plans to out me with his cut I had promised him. Rightfully so he could temporarily out me given I gave him enough supply to carry out his moves. However, he did not know that he killed the connection and all connections to him.

I drove to Chester wondering if he had the balls to venture to Honduras and make a connection himself. I had Carlos if I wanted to make another connection he still had Pablo; the gang was gone but Vanessa's brother was still breathing and working. I was just the East Coast supplier, Pablo still had everything I did not take in the West. Stilks never worked for me; he was just a business partner... he brought his work for the North Philly corners from me like everyone else in the city. Pete on Maine Street was wholesale and King Street was my store; I just owned both.

As we approached Estelle's house, my stomach curdled, the block was disgusting. I could smell the filth in the air... then before I opened my mouth to question Stilks knowledge; I quickly remembered the Choppers was ghetto dirty niggas. They flagged Kingston Jamaica hood-side but took the tin foil living with them. All that was missing was the goats and chickens running around in the open.

We sat parked on the corner that was located on the opposite side of the four-way intersection. Stalking the entrance of the house for about an hour before making a move. I had a third car following behind us on the road; it was Chancy, Scott, Dale and Brian... the only four I really trusted over everything. Chancy ran with Melly and me he always had my back and in my reality was always my right hand man I kept on tuck. The other three was my most valuable corner hoppers, closer to me then my own blood brothers. They helped me to surround Estelle's house.

Chancy was a goat for real, he ran through that alleyway, which was filled with empty chip bags, and bottles; newspapers, cats and piss and shit as if it was nothing. I already knew Jahgie was not there; I was able to confirm his moves because I had Omar's phone... the Choppers was sloppy; before I made up my mind to bait Dee and bag Estelle, I read the paper trail that was left on Omar's phone. While waiting for Stilks to give me his all clear on the Bridge Street take down. Omar fucked me over big time, Dee fucked up too but; Omar made shit worst.

I decided to take Stilks inside with me, even though I only asked for him to point Estelle out to me. Shit I wasn't stupid I had just given that man every reason to turn around and run on foot. I needed Carlos to keep watch over everything else, including Dee, who I had locked in the trunk of his car napping. After I whooped her naked ass and re-dressed her, I wasn't sure if was going to murk her after I had gotten what I needed or if I was going to forgive her and set her free, once I figured all the bull crap out.

Besides, I still needed her for bait. The streets wanted Dee more for snitching than they wanted me for being Kingpin. The Choppers was working hard to out me, their excitement was blowing up O's phone. When I didn't answer the first couple of phone calls, they started texting. Someone by the name Lee-lee texted first, after Jah's phone calls went to voice mail. Omar was so flamboyant and turtled he saved names to numbers. What started being a jigsaw puzzle with missing pieces was starting to become a map with a GPS guide. He earned me calling him a kindergarten cop; fucking turtle, slow motherfucker.

Lee-lee: "Omar, what's up Jah said everything is a go, did you get to Greg yet?"

Me: "Cool, I couldn't get to him; he had too many nigga around him, acting funny... but I got something better yall gonna be hype."

Lee-lee: "What? Don't fuck this shit up O; too much is riding on this."

Me: "What's up with the money?"

Lee-lee: "Ain't she cute?" then a picture followed the text, it was Journey; my heart melted, she has her mother gray eyes I thought, black long ponytails... damn baby girl is she mine I wondered... I don't know why I wanted her to be mine. Shit I was feeling like something good had to come from all this drama between Dee and me. I guess I wanted a reason for why I was riding for this girl who stopped riding for me. Dee stopped riding for me... however; I couldn't help but to notice the background of the picture.

Purple kitchen floors, and purple and white strip walls, with white cabinets with missing drawers. Who house was this, purple floors... where did I see these... I questioned myself. Meanwhile I decided to hold off the texting. Chancy was ready to kick in the door. With our guns drawn, Stilks, and I entered from the front while Chancy came in through the back, following Dale and Scott, we left Brian to watch Carlos. Estelle must have been in the kitchen cooking, she came running to the front door with a knife... Chancy kicked her in back she never saw his boot coming. "Lay down bitch... who else is in here?" Chancy yelled out...

"Go look I got this..." then as I stooped down to pick up the knife, with my gun pointed to her head I helped her to stand up to take a seat in the dining room chair. Stilks stayed with me while Chancy and Scott ran upstairs and Dale searched down the basement.

"It's just me nobody else Jahgie is not here... you want him right?" She cried out...

"My mamma told me to never trust a woman with gold teeth... so how can I trust you, to know you are alone?" I questioned...

"Omar, I thought he was with you? What do you want?"

"Omar? naw he not with Omar..." the bitch thought I was Omar, strange she knew him by name but not by face... Jackpot I thought she know something... and she wasn't Jamaican... everyone that know a Jamaican woman knows she for one is not talking and for two she is fighting. This girl was American and she was hurting.

"Are you looking for that baby he had? I had a bad feeling, I gave the baby to Lee-lee, Omar I do not have that baby, or your money. Jahgie left here the other day and I haven't seen him since."

"Where is Lee-lee, I didn't tell you to move nothing... did you get any orders from me to give the baby to Lee-lee?" I replied not knowing what was said...

"Lee-lee said she was bring her to you! Sal and that guy just came here looking for her..."

"What guy with him?"

"I don't know some old man... and Toby"

"Where did they go?"

"I don't know Jahgie said he was going to meet up with you and Sal got in the car with that guy..."

"What did the guy look like?"

"He was dark skin and he is African, he used to live near us in Cape Town, he comes from a rich family. I do not know why he is hanging with Sal... Sal is trouble. I keep telling Jahgie to leave him alone, but he is hard-headed..."

"Jahgie love you?"

"If this is love no..."

"We are friends of Jahgie; we are not going to hurt you... I didn't know who you was... my man kicked you because you came running at me with a knife. You don't know Omar when you see me?"

"No, we only spoke over the phone I don't remember seeing you in person..."

"So you called me by name like you knew me hun?"

"Jahgie told me you might come after me..."

"Why would I come after you?"

"Did you kill him for outing you?" she cried...

"Is he the only thug you banged?"

"What that's my brother..."

"Your brother... so you are Jamaican?"

"No, Sal is Jamaican we are African..."

"African? How old are you and where is the rest of your family?"

"Yes, my parents are still in Cape Town, South Africa... I am six-teen why... Is Jahgie in trouble?"

"Trouble ain't the word baby girl... do Omar a favor you like Omar right..."

"I don't know you look like you are going to kill me..."

"Nope unless you want me too... tell me was this the little girl..." then I showed her the picture Lee-lee sent to Omar's phone.

"Yeah, Journey she is a smart little girl, she talk too much for me though... didn't you see her?"

"Nope, where is your phone? Do you have a phone?"

"Right there on the table..." then Dale reached over and passed it to me while everyone else stood in position quiet.

"Call Jahgie and tell him Omar called looking for him, and put it on speaker for me..." then as her dumb ass was told she called him... wow Omar was really a turtle. He was so busy trying to fuck me over that he didn't realize the Choppers was playing him the whole time; damn he sold me out for a bullet in his head... just when I wanted to have some sympathy for him... I was glad his bullets came from me. Omar deserved all seven of them...

"What's up Essie?" he answered...

"Omar called me looking for you..." she commented without the tears...

"Omar called you, but he didn't answer when I called him..."

"Yes, he just called me... what's going on Jahgie you told me everything was going to be okay..."

"Get out of the house, go to the train station and wait for me there..." I shook my head no; as she raised hers to look at me...shit a camera trap I thought, too many people...

"What's wrong?"

"Get to the train station I will be there in five minutes hurry up..." then he hung up the phone...

"You fucked up baby girl; he is coming here ain't he?"

"I don't know... he said the train station..."

"Men let's rock out, you grab her... she is riding with us..." I pointed to Stilks who was looking upset and clueless...we left out the back door; and ran through the dirty alleyway quickly into our cars. I now had two human baits on hand. One for Sal and one for Jahgie... I needed Mr. Stilks for one other favor... his fuming ass was just going to be a mad ass...We drove to

136

Juniper Street, the last place the Choppers would come looking.

Carlos pulled into the garage, because he had to let Dee out of the trunk. Shit the neighbors was probably watching with their looking asses. Carlos owned two workhouses on Juniper Street; one was the place where Vanessa kept the worker kids. That was on the opposite side of the block, it used to be a dirty as hell in there. Likewise, the other was across the street on the corner. Uptown blocks are small and the houses have either third floors or two floors.

The other house had two floors, but the kid house had crawl spaces and a third floor. More than enough room to hide during a gunfight. I had to come up with a plan quick but I needed to sort things out with Dee first. My head was spinning connecting the dots. Then as I pulled Dee to the side, Dale turned on the TV...

Chapter 14

Game Changer

"**B**reaking news, the New Jersey State police is searching for the owners of a property in the Alpine section of the Garden State tonight, in connection to a possible house invasion that occurred on Tuesday morning sometime around midnight. A body was found in an upstairs bedroom, police believe the man found was a gunman they are not sure if he was murdered in self-defense or what the case may be. However, what police want the public to be on the lookout for is, something the investigation team is calling disturbing... more on what they found in that mansion. Here is Officer Baily with more information he spoke today at a conference hosted by other officials." The reporter stated... Damn, that was my house I thought to myself...

"We want the neighbors to be alarmed about the crime that took place here in Alpine on Tuesday morning; we are not sure if this was an isolated crime or the start of something else. Our side of town does not know this type of crime, the district and I are working none stop to see that the person or persons responsible for what happened is caught; before we can release the name of the victim found, we want to find the owners, who neighbor's say lived in the property.

We are looking for Gregory Weston, a known felon from the Philadelphia area, and Deandra Harper a known girlfriend to Weston. Both have ties to the Philadelphia, area and New Jersey. Sources say these two also have ties to the notorious El Pablo gang; Deandra Harper is, also known as Christa Valery the daughter of ex-Philadelphia policer Antonio Jameson, who was arrested in Philadelphia a few years ago; on unrelated charges.

We are not sure, if this has anything to do with what happened to Jameson, or if this is something different. A neighbor, who was walking their dog around midnight, heard what sounded like gunshots or a bomb blowing up inside the residence. When police arrived, they found the body of a male in the bedroom upstairs.

The forensic team was brought in yesterday afternoon to begin their investigation. There has been no sign of the couple who, is believed to have been in the home. Other sources told police Harper/Valery no longer resides in the resident; however, the county records still have her name on the Deed to the property. Earlier today, a team of special officers went back into the home with forensic with a search warrant to search for clues to the whereabouts of Mr. Weston, he nor Harper/Valery are suspects at the time, Just persons of interest and no charges have been filed.

We just want to know what happened or if they know anything about what happened. Officers are not one-hundred percent sure, the owners was home during the time of the invasion. This is a gated property, and the owners could have not been there. Family for neither party have been reachable by authorities. No missing person's reports was filed! Nor, has one been attempted to be filed as of yet in the State of New Jersey...

Police did find a hidden bunker located under the homes foundation. Officers searching the property tried to track a blood trail that led to a door inside of the bunker. Officers have reported finding illegal firearms and military style weapons inside the bunker. The bomb squad was called-in, to remove grenades that were found stored in boxes. As a precaution neighbors in the cul-de-sac was evacuated temporarily. My men and I have never seen this amount of ammunition in a civilian's possession before. Authorities are still not sure if anyone was living in the bunker or held against their will. It also looks like a child or children had been living in the home as well, we want to find if this evidence was true or if the child or children co-lived in the home.

We are asking for the public's help in identifying the Victim and if anyone have information about the crime or persons of interest please contact police. Do not attempt to address neither one yourself they are presumed to be armed and dangerous... More information will be provided as the investigation continues... we are asking the persons of interest to please turn yourselves into police... here is Officer O'Malley from Cleveland who has something to add to what we are calling a murder mystery."

"On behalf of the State of Ohio, we are taking on the search for these two persons of interest along with Philadelphia City and New Jersey. Harper/ Valery, was last seen in Ohio visiting an inmate at Mt Holly women's Penitentiary in Cleveland. The inmate is not cooperating with authorities, we will not be releasing the inmate's name at this time; she is not a person of interests.

Sam's Diner a few miles from the jail, has video we are reviewing of Harper/ Valery dining with a group of people on Tuesday afternoon; following her visit with the female inmate. We are not sure at this time who are the other people seen in the tape that joined Harper/ Valery at the dinner. However, we do know ABC reporter Kathy Armstrong was among the group dinning with Harper/ Valery. Officers in New York have taken Armstrong in for questioning.

This will be an ongoing investigation as stated. Harper/ Valery was seen leaving with Gregory Weston, he was also among the group dining at Sam's. Sources say the two left Armstrong and the others in the group stranded... ABC has yet to make a statement on Armstrong's behalf in the case. Covington police department found a black Jeep floating in Devou Park River in Covington today.

It matches the vehicle the one witnesses say Weston and Harper/ Valery drove off in; the pair was not found in the Vehicle. It appears that either, Weston and Harper/ Valery dumped the car or others may be involved. Ohio do not have a felony crime in connection to what happened to New Jersey, however our officers will join forces with New Jersey. It is a misdemeanor in the State of Ohio to dump personal property illegally. The Jeep is registered under Driveme.com car rental services; they tell us Armstrong signed the release papers with the rental service...however, the car was not reported stolen.

Although no fingerprints were found on the Jeep and the license plate and stickers have been removed; this is a signs the car was indeed dumped. An arrest warrant has been issued for Gregory Weston, and Deandra Harper also known as Christa Valery. I would like to introduce Officer Fallen head detective for Philadelphia."

"This is a federal investigation with jurisdiction in three states; we know so far our persons of interest have crossed and are together. We are not saying crimes by the pair was committed in all three states, New Jersey has the body. We know these two individuals have ties to our city, so we will do what is in our power to help our neighbors. Please do not try to apprehend these two; the districts are not sure if they are armed and dangerous or just people we need to speak too. Call the police if you see them. Do not approach them, walk away and call the police." Damn I thought...

"We will have more information about the search for Weston and his accomplice tonight coming up at ten, with David Sowers who will be reporting live from Alpine New Jersey. More breaking news back in Philadelphia, NBC's Stephen Mc'Coffy is live in North Philadelphia, where fighter fighters are battling a five-alarm fire on the 1000 block of Memphis in the Fish Town section of the city. Stephen..." The news inquirer stated...

"Tonight Philadelphia police have their hands full... a five-alarm blaze took the lives of ten people and counting, in the 1000 block of Memphis Street this afternoon. Neighbors who talked to us do not want to be identified; say the homes belonged to a drug lord who moved to town a few months ago. They have been fighting for the city to shut these homes down... Neighbors are upset and want answers... an eyewitness was taken in for questioning today they told authorities the homes had been fire bombed.

After gunfire was traded between the ringleader who had setup shop in the city months ago and another rivaling party. No one has been named in connection to this sad situation; we are calling this the Memphis Blaze. All of the victims are believed to be adults their names have not been released the authorities are working to identify all of the victims at this time, and their relatives.

No fire fighters have been reported injured, two however was taken in for observation for smoke inhalation... the fire Chief say they had to call in for help from three other nearby districts to help put out the inferno. The Simon Hill recreation center located down the street was placed on locked-down; they are hosting summer camp, and the director told me earlier that all parents was notified to pick up their children; who had just came inside for lunch.

Other children who was on the playground say they had to run for their lives, while others told me they had to hit the deck! A term used for dropping to the floor, when bullets fly through the air; considering they have no names. We are working to gather more information for our viewers coming up at ten-o'clock. Back to you Stacey..." then as the drama went on I was praying not to be connected with the fire too.

"Tonight we are covering a shooting that claimed the lives of three in the South West section overnight... Police were called to the scene around four this morning, to where reports were called in about gunshots heard coming from King Street. When the Police arrived, they found twenty- five year old Alileemah Fernand, lying in the middle of the street shot multiple times in her chest. She was rushed to the Hospital where died in the ambulance.

The body of Twenty-nine year old Pearson Lopez was found on the corner of Stiles street, Police believe he tried to run home to where he collapsed on the sidewalk. His body was found when the Police went to block the street off. Another male found has yet to be identified he was lying next to the two other unidentified victims and he pronounced dead at the scene... his body was sent to the medical examiner's office. The other two victims, were rushed to the University Hospital, and are listed in critical condition; under police guard; their names have not been released." Damn strike three... all three news highlights was about us... I was just wondering how long it was going to take them to connect the dots...

"Look this shit just got real we have to change the game plan and burn all the tracks that follow us. Fuck the FED's is on to us, we have to throw them off track..." I replied in response to the media broadcast.

"Gee, believe it or not but you and Dee is going to have to clear yall names, before we go any further..." Carlos added...

"Naw, I trailed blood when we escaped."

"Then Dee you go clear your name..."

"I can't the body was my bodyguard."

"Hold up what is going on here?" Scott questioned...

"Look a lot of shit went down, let me come clean...Omar sold me out to the Choppers, the Choppers in return sold out Omar who used Dee to get to me... Omar and myself was Pete..."

"Hold up homie you was Pete?" Dale questioned...

"Listen..." I yelled, but no one was listening, instead they drew their guns on me all except Estelle and Dee, who was unarmed; Estelle was tied up in the trunk of my car, and Carlos, Chancy and Stilks stood by my side.

"Nigga you had us out here trapping for you while Pete had us starving... you are a grimy nigga... fuck you..." Scott replied, before Chancy shot both him and Dale... it happened so fast, that they never had a chance to pull their triggers. Damn bull's-eye...

"As long as we know what is going on those two are irrelevant... Kingpin, don't ever explain yourself to a peasant. You are the king of these streets... fuck the police, prove to the streets that you earned this shit..." then without warning Chancy, shot Carlos twice...pop-pop...

"Why Carlos, Chancy?" I asked... the look on Dee and Stilks faces was priceless... Chancy was a goat...he never hated on me. It should have been, Melly, me and Chancy and his pop Chauncey. Chauncey was killed a few years back, fucking around with those Hispanics...after we robbed Carlos cash house. My senses tell me Carlos had something to do with it.

"Carlos been on his phone all day diming you out and you didn't see it...why is he so eager to help you? You took his spot. He knew Omar sent Jasper to look for you on Plover Street. Ever since he got out of jail, he been looking for Jeff to clear his name. When you was down the docks waiting for Stilks Carlos told whomever he was talking too you fell for it... whatever it was didn't seem like he had your back. Besides, I owe that fat motherfucker! Get over it and open your eyes we got into this shit together and baby boy we are going out together... fuck your daddy, he is working with the DA to get you... I hate cops... fat fucking pig..." Damn I had to scratch my head on that note...

"Daddy?" Dee shouted...

"Long story, baby girl... Stilks I need another favor..." damn, my mind went blank it was just too much...

"Greg..." Dee shouted...

"Not now bitch shut up!" I yelled back to her...

"A million year hun?" sighed Stilks...

"Taking or walking?" I replied... holding my hands out in disbelief...

"After I find my wife and daughter I am done doing favors for you! I want out Greg!" A part of me wanted to say if you find your wife and kid... instead I knotted and changed up the game plan... by this time it was after seven- thirty in the evening. Dee was able to identify the background in the picture of her daughter... Stilks went with Chancy to clean up the bodies. I still had Estelle in the trunk, I didn't want to scare Dee any more then what I had already done, therefore I didn't tell her. After Chancy came back with Stilks, the six of us drove to southwest to pay Kaliyah a visit. The psychedelic kitchen belonged to Kaliyah's mother.

Chapter 15
Because of a bitch

On the search to find Journey, hoping Kaliyah still had her in her custody. I approached the corner of her mother's block, only to cross paths with my son. I spotted him out of four children who had been wondering the streets unaccompanied by an adult. As he walked closer to the car I was sitting in, to cross the street to go to the nearby corner store; I could not help but to find myself looking at myself. Before speaking a word to my partners, I sat at the light in traffic, wondering what type of mother would allow her child to roam the streets at night alone.

Makhi Geovanni Jones-Weston, rumbled through my mind as I tried to figure out another plot in this twisted situation. He looked just like me; he had my walk down to the swag. Chancy fucked my mindset up... although Carlos and my relationship was mostly business, I respected him, and I always felt like he cared for me. He was the father the streets never knew I had. In front of my face the only person who knew Carlos was my father, shot him dead in my face. I did nothing to help him; the glare in his eyes was starting to disturb me. Dee hated him; I knew she didn't feel anything. For once, I was lost for words... I felt like I was stuck in the same circle Dee claimed to have been trapped in...

How could I allow my resentment towards Kaliyah divide me from an innocent child, who did not ask to be here? In that moment I was starting to see the traits I inherited from my own father. I was also starting to realize what Alison was asking me... why Dee, why would I allow her to control my personal life. Alison told me "bad bitches bring men down, they break us into pieces; good women build men into good people." In returned I asked her, "why me?" she replied... "Past the evil I see a man fighting to heal what hurts..." Alison is married now... she left me alone because I could not let go of Dee. Damn something good has to come of this... I hated soaking in my feelings; they got the best of me.

"Brian take Stilks with you and go over there in the arcade and give all the kids in there one hundred dollars each in quarters. Make sure none of them leaves out have Stilks guard the door. Here take this... Yo especially the one right there in the yellow Polo shirt; watch him with your life..." I passed him a fist full of money, Dee was sitting in the front seat looking at me funny.

"Yo boss that's my nephew...." Stilks said as he leant over the driver side door.

"Then go be uncle Stilks and make sure he don't leave..." I replied...

"Listen man, what are you about to do, you didn't say nothing about no kids man. What you think you are Carlos now? I don't know about this..."

"Do you want the double or no? All you have to do is watch the kids, so I won't have to turn into Carlos... fuck this up and I am going to let Chancy fuck you up."

"Alright man don't play with me like that, I am just saying..."

"You ain't saying shit man go handle what I told you too..." then as Brian pulled Stilks away, I rolled up my window and drove around the corner to come up the block from the other way.

"Dee, you ready?" I asked...

"Yup what's the move?"

"Go ask for Kaliyah..."

"Give me the gun..." this was the Dee I loved gangster... I passed her a nine... Chancy and I watched as she walked up the steps and rang the doorbell. Hopefully Kaliyah would give Dee Journey. Hopefully, they could see eye-to-eye... damn...

Part 4

Gridlock

I rang the doorbell twice... my mind was blank and my heart felt hurt. I felt torn between the streets and my family. Greg didn't tell me what it was he knew. He was just calling shoots and killing whoever stepped in his way. All I knew was whose kitchen my daughter was sitting in. Ms. Valetta never met my daughter, and neither did Kaliyah to my knowledge. I was hoping my daughter was not in that house. Then just as Ms. Valetta came to open the door, I took a deep breath; exhaling my fears.

"Hello, is Kaliyah here?" I asked holding my head low to the ground.

"Who is asking?" a female other than Ms. Valetta questioned...

"D..." then before I could say Dee, Ms. Valetta came up from behind her...

"Who is it Dena?" she shouted all while pulling the door open wider...

"Is Kaliyah here?" I asked again...

"Deandra, what are you doing here? You are not welcomed to my house anymore, I do not know what you and Kaliyah got going on but do not be bring no trouble to my door."

"Ms. Valetta, I am not coming to bring no trouble, I need to talk to Kaliyah... its important..."

"What's important, is you leaving... you are not welcome here bitch..." then as I looked to my left I could see Greg pulling off, my heart skipped a beat...

"Bitch, what did I ever do to you? I haven't seen Kaliyah in years... I just want to say hello...please let me talk to her if she is here. I do not want no trouble... I swear!"

"You heard her go head girl step before I make you step..." Dena said pushing her way back into the doorway.

"You ain't going to do shit to me... tell me where I can find Kaliyah and I will leave..."suddenly gunshots made a crowd of people run in our direction, scattering...

"Oh my fucking God, my grandkids are out there... Kaliyah they shooting outside... Kaliyah yall come on they are shooting... girl move..." Valetta screamed to the top of her lungs. As Valetta and Dena rushed past me, I brushed passed her as she pushed me into the door to move out of her way.... Kaliyah came running from the basement with Sal following behind. My life flashed before my eyes as I came face to face with Sal and Kaliyah. I was alone staring at two of the millions of enemies that followed me. I was the streets most wanted, my best friend been on my shit list, since she fucked my man. She and my ex put a price on my head.

My mouth dropped, I was dumbstruck. My heart broke into yet another piece. Kaliyah was wearing my daughter's neckless. I gave Journey a diamond neckless with a diamond nameplate that read... "Heirs", it was a birthday gift. I thought the worst.

"Kaliyah, where is my daughter?" I yelled...

"I don't have your fucking daughter bitch... what are you doing here?"

"Sal you looking for me? Give me back my family..." I yelled... Sal eyes cringed in anger. I was familiar with his tactics, I used to be afraid of him; he was a bully. I guess I grow up! I wasn't frightened any more... Greg beat my ass in that car; I had to prove to him that I was innocent. I never saw this person Kaliyah turned into... the clock felt like it stopped... I blacked out seeing nothing but that same wicked vision I drifted off into; when Mona flashed before my eyes. Only difference was the black and white maze was now closing in on me. It was a two on one rumble.

Punching, and swinging, I was fighting for my life. Kaliyah swung first; I slammed her chubby body onto the living room glass table. I remember hearing the glass breaking, as Sal jumped in grabbing me by ponytail. I fell to my knees;

Kaliyah jumped up and tackled me. I could not reach for my gun, which fell deep into my underwear. The three of us was tussling back and forth. Sal was choking me, whispering, "Consider this as our makeup... didn't' I tell you not to fuck with the Sensations. Oh, boy the Choppers is going to love this. Go to sleep... go to sleep... Ashanti... you thought I didn't recognize my pretty face... where is Greg... I can kill him but you... somebody else wants you..." I back kicked him so hard, and flipped him over my shoulders. He fell holding his nuts.

Kaliyah on the other hand waited for me to lean over the breakfast bar. I was holding my neck trying to catch my breath. I thought she was down. I could see Sal trying to stand to his feet; he was pulling himself up holding onto the arm of couch. She tackled me; I hit my head on the wall. Once she got me onto the floor, she managed to drag me my legs. I had no strength.

Kaliyah pulled me down the basement steps; Sal was still laying on the floor, I was kicking hard. Her grip was strong. All of a sudden, I heard someone screaming my name...

"Dee... Dee...." He yelled... I could not speak... I was dizzy... my head hit a nail that was coming out of the bottom of the steps... she threw me into a closet. I was gridlocked...

Chapter 16

Bullets have no names

I drove around the corner leaving Dee on the doorsteps of Kaliyah mother's house. She was taking too long to come back to the car; I feared the worst. I shot at the tree around the corner in the park that was behind the house to create a diversion. I sent Chancy to go after her. Brian and Stilks still had the arcade on lock. I saw Kaliyah running right past me. I followed her, she was running in the same direction of the arcade. My phone ringed...

"Yo they locked us in here boss..." damn it was Brian calling to tell me the arcade owners locked everyone inside the building.

"Yo stay cool we got this... don't let yellow shit out of your sight..."

"What about Stilks I don't see him..."

"What... where did he go?"

"I don't know man..." fuck I thought, Stilks stiffed us...

"Sit tight... watch yellow shirt..."

"He not here B..."

"Are you kidding me?" fucking fuck...

"Get out man..." I hung up quickly...

I reached for my other gun that was in the back seat in one of the duffel bags I had loaded with ammunition. Cops sirens was starting to show their cars...I drove off to a small block away from the park. The park started filling up with police presents. The police focused on the wrong side, as they swarmed the basketball outdoor court, looking for a shooter. There was a basketball game going on at the time; the tensions was high, the courts was jam-packed with players and watchers... I ran right up to Kaliyah...

"What up Seek...you look like you just seen a ghost..."

"Greg..." she was shock to see me I could tell... I grabbed her by her face pinching her cheeks together. I shoved her to a gate that was in front of someone's house.

"Get off me..." she muttered...

"Where is my son at dirty?"

"Greg I never been dirty... get off me! Oh now you want to claim my son... fuck you Greg..."

"Yup, your food stamps say he is mine ... so where is he... I want to meet him..."

"So you are going to hit his mother? I am going to go get him now! Didn't you hear them over there shooting...?"

"Naw, I just pulled up, about to run in the store. And I pinched you; I didn't hit you... why are you looking all crazy. Your hair is all over the place, your shirt is torn. Are you snorting now? You look bad Seek" I was playing cool; I always talked to her like that...

"Stop playing with me, if you took care of your son like you said you would... I would not have had to go get food stamps."

"I did my part... what did you do smoke it... what this in your hair? It that glass?" I said picking glass out of her hair...

"I was fighting; the only person on drugs is your crack-head mother."

"We never got that deep you don't know my mother... so cool it with the childish jokes. Who was you fighting?" I wanted to hit her so bad...but there was people sitting on their step across from us.

"Some girl in the bar hit me with a bottle..."

"You are still a hood rat... you used to be too pretty for that. If I didn't know you I probably would have wifed you. That ass been on fleek...but you scheme too much for me...you still bang with the Sensations? Where that crazy ass Sal at? I need to holla at him..."

"You had your own hood rat. My scheming was good enough to work for you wasn't it... you been trying to get this kitty ever since I let you hit it..." then she showed me her Sensation's tattoo on her hand.

"So where is Sal I got some work for him, Omar did his thing with this drop... Pete gave us a good deal."

"I don't know he around...Omar what's up with him? I heard he is going crazy since that King Street shizzle went down last night Southwest is off the hook. I am about to get my kids out of here...can we stay with you?" she said laughing...

"With me, naw... out here I can fuck with the Sensations, that's business...but I can't bring yall home... Uptown is still me..."

"Where you live in Uptown? Stop lying Omar said you moved to Connecticut, that's why you been M.I.A!"

"Naw... he lied..."

"Yo who is Pete?" by this time we had reached the corner near the store, which was in the middle of the block. Then before we could finish our introductions, Valetta came walking down the street with some big lady, three of Kaliyah's other kids, and some other kids... all of whom I saw walking into the arcade... Yellow shit wasn't among the crew...

"Kaliyah, you over here talking and we couldn't find Makhi nowhere... Lee-lee is on her way over to the house now...Stilks had found him playing the arcade. He was in there treating the kids. He is bring him back now... come on girl get your kids... hey Greg long time no see. Give my grandson some money... he is getting ready to go to Dena house with the kids. How you been, that Dee was just at my house looking for Kaliyah. Yall together?"

"No... she got married, Dee don't fuck with me anymore. You, didn't tell me you saw Dee... what she want?"

"I was in the bar...I didn't see her!"

"No, that was her wasn't you in the basement with Sal, when I told you they was out here shooting?" Kaliyah gave Valetta this stare... I panicked...Chancy was calling me in code... call hang up, call, hang up, call hang up... code for assistance out front four calls would have been out back...

"Oh shit..." I replied, pushing Kaliyah who was standing in my face... Valetta grabbed my shirt as I tried to run. I pushed her.

"Damn, Greg it's like that?" Valetta yelled...

"Naw, not now stay over here... I'll be right back... stay here..." Kaliyah was on my heels. As I ran towards her block, she changed direction and ran the back way.

"Brian where is Chancy and Dee?" I said brushing paths with Brian who was running from the other direction...

"There go Stilks!" He shouted! Stilks eyes lit up when he saw us coming. He was trying to jostle Natalie back into the car she pulled up in... tossing yellow shirt into the back seat... he proceeded to rush across the street where I was running into his direction with his gun pointed at us. Brian and I drew our guns in return...

"Put your gun down Stilks..."

"Naw man, all due respect I can't do it... you are out of control..." he replied...

"Stilks don't play Nigga... your bitch crossed you not me..." His love hard feelings for Natalie was deep. He forgot love and the street code don't mix. Natalie opened the driver's door; talking shit taking her man back...

"Gee, I can't let you do it...that's my family..."

"Stilks we cool man... watch out!" Neither Stilks nor Natalie saw Jahgie running behind them as Stilks and I stood golden corral style in the middle of the two-lane street. Jahgie shot Stilks, before I could. Fuck my son was in the car... Stilks fell to the ground in front of yellow shit who was peeking out the window from the back seat... Jahgie grabbed, Natalie as a shield; and all hell broke loose. He started shooting across the car at Brian and me. I grabbed Brian and we rolled on the ground crawling behind a car...

"Fuck I'm out..." I said... checking the bullets in my pistol.

"He coming go, I got you…" Brian rolled to the back of the car and started sacking off. I rolled to another car and slouched between the two-parked cars. Brian was still going hard, he reloaded his gun. Suddenly a third gun fired. Screams slithered the night skies… I looked up and it was Chancy. He ran right up to Jahgie and shot him! He fell on top of Natalie.

"Let's rock out… we got one…" Chancy shouted… I ran to the car to see if Journey was inside of it… fuck it wasn't her… damn yellow shirt clutched his body over top of the another little girl's body. He didn't look up to see me staring in the window. I fucked up… and I knew it… Somebody ran to the lifeless bodies… Natalie got up screaming…

"I am not hit…I am not hit…"Brian, Chancy and I ran out of harm's way! I could hear spectators screaming.

"Chancy where is Dee?" I questioned trying to catch my breath…I was limping like shit… it felt like that bullet Dee shot me with was still in my thigh… I was hoping the stitches didn't pop… I was doing too much.

"I don't know she wasn't in there I got Sal tied up in your trunk… I pistol whipped him…"

"So where was Dee Chancy?" I repeated as we were running.

"I am telling you she wasn't in there man…"

"I'm hit yall…" Brian commented…

"Here at man…" Chancy said…

"My vest... damn... my vest...that was close."

Chapter 17

I'll Spit on Your Grave

"You thought you did something hun? Why me?" I finally got myself together on my own I hid in the alleyway on the side of the yard between the neighbor's trashcans. I approached Kaliyah as she came running down the alleyway...

"You tell me Dee you came looking for me..."

"Tell me where Jahgie and Sal is holding my daughter and husband at..."

"What are you talking about? How dare you come to my mother's house with your fucking drama... the judge gave me two years... I did two years in jail for you. My son's father don't want nothing to do with him... because of you... but you don't get it... everything isn't about you Dee!"

"First you fuck my man, you get pregnant by him, you keep it... knowing it would hurt me... why do you have my daughters neckless around your neck?"

"Sal gave me this neckless, to give to our daughter... I didn't want to lose it... its not yours..."

"I know what I gave my daughter... where is she?"

"I don't know what you are talking about... what happened why would you think I have your daughter?"

"Someone sent Omar a picture of my daughter sitting in your kitchen... I know Valetta's poverty stricken decorations when I see them..."

"Wow, you always thought you was better than everyone else. Mona had you eating out of trashcans, and selling your pussy for beepers... your coochie made a come up and suddenly the price goes up. You are no different from me. Tell me do you remember what struggling feels like?"

"I do and I am looking at the struggle now...why Greg?"

"Why not Greg? I hit jackpot Dee... or so I thought... do you want to know why Sal too? One word jackpot...Boo!" She crushed my heart with her mocking laughter.

"I get it Kaliyah, but I am selfish... I am sorry you feel that way... do you remember the list?"

"What list?"

"1. No pussy without money... Do not take less than sneaker money $30 minimum. Pussy costs never forget that.

2. Hush money is always doubled and do not stop until you get everything you want and do not want...

3. Always use a condom no matter what, if he wants to hit raw he has to pay extra. If he does not like it, you say fuck you pay me and you add his bill up or you scream I am telling.

4. Tell him to get you a beeper and he has to pay the bill.

5. No kissing you do not know who pussy he been licking.

6. If you sucking dick never let him cum in your mouth and dick sucking is extra, cum-super-soaking is extra, extra and remember sucking dick really turn men on and a good blow-job will always give you the upper hand...

7. Never, fall in love with anyone you just fucking for mutual funds...

8. If he is not filling your pockets regularly, then never catch feelings and do not ever let me catch you fighting no bitch over a Nigga...

9. Don't ever sweat a man let him jock you...and...

10. Friends do not snitch on friends you are my sister, and we are not going to bite each other backs..." I remembered that fuck you pay me list she had written for us some years ago... it was the bond we was to live by...

"Dee you are crazy... who long ago was that?"

"You broke seven, eight and ten... we never thought about adding an eleventh rule... eleven should have been... Never sleep with one another lovers, boyfriends or something like that... there is no neutral..."

"What are you talking about bitch go head before I fuck you up again... you are lucky I gave two fucks..."

"For the record I didn't put you in jail. You put yourself in that cage...who got my daughter Kaliyah stop lying I know she was here..."

"She was here, but I don't have her, Sal been gave her to Jahgie..." She stole my daughters neckless and helped to fuckup my life... I pulled my glock nine out and I pointed it to her head.

"On your knees... don't move... where is Jahgie now with my daughter?"

"Dee I didn't do nothing to her... I am sorry Dee... come on I just wanted to do better by my kids... Dee we are better than this...." She cried...

"Why Kaliyah, who was behind all of this shit... why set the price and why me why Greg... you played me. You wanted to walk in my shoes so bad; you ruined our friendship. My sister, closer to me than my own blood. You knew if I was up so was you... I never turned my back on you... I would have given you the clothes off my back. You fucked my ex not like I love him, but you knew about our relationship. You Kaliyah, not me... it was you... this is crazy. Do you know what I've been through in the last two days? I thought when I left the street niggas alone that I brunt all the shit that hurt.

There is no wonder I cannot move on...life my nigga... I can't continue to be buried alive in this skin of mine. Because of you... we was bad bitches.... We had the men with the money, designer clothes... cars... trips... the haters. We not just me, I tried to pull you on my team, I tried to help you. I faked it to make it and I made it; I wanted you to make it. As much as I hate Mona... Mamma was right about you. She warned me to stay away from you. Mamma told me... She didn't like you! For the life of me, I didn't understand what she was saying to me.

Hell, Mamma didn't care for me much. You are right; I did have to eat garbage the nights Mamma did not feed me. Yeah she beat me... she broke me. I resent her still may God rest her soul, and forgive her for her sins. If only I had listen to Mamma and not you...her words haunt me Kaliyah. They hurt... She would say Deandra that girl is a bad influence, and I do not want you to turn out like her. I had your back. No matter how wrong Greg was... he was so right...

I know now why he pushed me away; it wasn't just because he fucked you, or because you had his baby. I was young then... I was numb... I saw yall on the couch on Washington Ave. the dick was not worth the hype was it. He pounded you like a two-dollar hooker. Boo, what made the hype worth my wild... is the mare fact Greg made love to me. He took his time thrusting his penis on me clitoris. Thirty-second miles of pumping. You moaned and you acted a fool. Had the nerve to smile in my face at my graduation, and followed us to the party.

What, you came to tell my man your baby was his? You wasn't there to support me... to busy hating on me... my sister told me, when you saw her, you asked about me. Then when she told you I was married and I moved to Africa with my husband... no my rich husband, you told her that it wouldn't last long. Because I did not deserve it. What happen to saying congratulations... whether you were happy for me not?

You said you would be there for me; I kept my end of the stick. If I would have known your son was Greg's, I would have made sure he was taken care of... we would have said fuck Greg together. I never been on some me shit! You told Sal about me! The letters that came to your house from him to me... you only gave me one. Kaliyah you told me he never wrote back... you wrote him back!"

"It wasn't supposed to go down like this Dee... I was just there I did not have nothing to do with it... Sal did it, he want the streets back. He robbed Greg's distribution house on Maine Street. Omar told him too, Jahgie switched up the game plan... this had nothing to do with you... it was between the Southwest Sensations and the Uptown Boys... Jahgie brought in the Choppers..."

"You are a Chopper! So where is my fucking daughter and my fucking husband?"

"I was a Southwest Sensation... I am done with that life. I did not see your husband; they just gave me the baby...Jahgie, and Craig have her... damn Dee! I don't know where they are at!"

"Where is she?" I repeated again...then she looked at...with tears in her eyes...

"8. Do not ever let me catch you fighting no bitch over a Nigga..." Kaliyah caught me off guard, she must have saw the startled look in my eyes... she jumped up and head-butted me to the ground. The gun flow somewhere behind me. The two of us was back tussling back and forth it was life or death. We were both giving it to each other. Blow for blow! She was struggling to grab my pistol. I was pulling her by her leg. Somehow, I was able to grab the gun from out of her hand. She was holding if backwards. Fumbling to point it in my direction.

I snatched it... I snatched it... I snatched it... I pulled the trigger. Kaliyah laid on the ground gasping for air... I shot her at close-range... one time in the stomach. Damn that shit hurt...

"Dee, please don't...," she cried...

"Where is my daughter?"

"Fuck you Dee... I told you I do not have her... I told you Jahgie and Craig have her..."

"You ruined my life you know that... give me my daughter's neckless..." I then snatched Journeys neckless off Kaliyah's neck, she crunched... as I proceeded to walk away...

"Don't leave me here.... help... help... I am sorry... help...help..." she tried to scream...

"Kaliyah, I'm sorry... how could we let chicken change and men come between us? I won't leave you like this...bad bitches stick together," I cried out, my heart was hurting... I never would have thought Kaliyah and I would let a gang divide us...

"Dee... please help me... we are better than this... don't leave me here... help me... Dee..." she was breathing harder and harder, after each word she wheezed out...

"That's why needed an eleventh rule... you know 7/11... If I roll a 1 or a 2, or a 3; a 10 I lose... a 7 or 11 would make us neutral... craps... damn I'm sorry..." I cried out, I didn't know what to say or what to do...

"Dee... please go get some help... don't come to my grave, with your tears... don't pray for my soul when you are sitting up in your cell at night. You let me die and I will haunt you..." She cried as blood surfed out of her mouth.

"You want my help or not... how can I trust you..." Then as I went to hold her hand... feeling sorry for what I had done... she squeezed my hand tight.

"You are going to let me die I know it! Tommy smashed me good, wish I would have heard that hype... strike three Sensations won! Thought I was going to take that to my grave... your husband was good boo. You married the enemy." Soaking in her own blood, she whispered... then she purposely hawed spitted, blood in my face... laughing out loud... as she coughed up more blood...

"I won't cry... but I will spit on your grave..." I shot her again... I stared for a second as her eyes rolled to the back of her head.

Chapter 18

Loves Curse

I ran for my life. I was trembling. I was crying. I ran to the same dead-end street behind the old oil refinery; a few blocks away for Kaliyah's house; Sal used to take me too. My top shirt had blood on it. I had to dump my clothes. I searched through the trash that was dumped in the vacant lot... hoping to find something to put on to cover my vest. No matter how hard I was trying to shake what had just happened from my mind. I couldn't... I slid my body between the dumpster and an old pissy mattress, which was leaning against it.

My tears was warm, I did not let out a sound. Dreading someone would hear me, even though I was alone. Loves curse was haunting me yet again. Four years and a baby I wasn't sure of the father... my mind pivoted to one of the happiest times of my life. The hallucination was so clear...

August 1st... I flew to New York with Thomas from Las Vegas, on his private jet. The two of us could not keep our hands off each other. We earned points for the mile-high club. It was my rebirth, the start of life without Greg. I was not supposed to look back. I was supposed to stay focused. Thomas... Thomas... changed right before my eyes. I fell for his authenticity. Our wedding was small, but the train on my gown was long. I wore white, even though I had already given birth to Journey.

"I accept your past, but I feel like you need to close that chapter in your life, so I can open up new doors with you. Take time and explore with you. I know we haven't known each other for a long time and there are still millions of things we still need to learn about each other...but I am ready to build this relationship with you, just like my father built his empire; brick and hand..." Thomas words spoke to me ...

"No you didn't woman, all jokes aside, I just told you I found my soul mate, I didn't say I think, I said from the moment we met I felt like we were meant to be. If you weren't meant to be my wife then maybe you were meant to be my best friend. But we were meant to meet...I am a man of family values... the woman that I marry won't have to worry about me reaching out to another woman for friendship. She wouldn't have to worry about me going out looking to sow my royal oats. I said I want to give you all of me; nonetheless, I want you to do the same." Damn we cheated each other...

It was our last night in New York, and I was stumbling my feet to pack. I really did not want to leave, but I did not want to stay knowing I had to release my past and let go of my baggage. It would have been unbiased, if I brought stones to a glass house. I really did not want to pack; I did not want to leave Thomas... I did not want to leave him. Stones to a glass house. Glasshouse... Stones to a glass house. Glasshouse... Stones to a glasshouse. Glasshouse... Stones to a glasshouse. Glasshouse...

"I don't like making promises, but I like you enough to step out on faith and see where this friendship can go. But you are going to stop fucking me like that though for real... where did you learn them tongue tricks from?" wow... I thought... Stones to a glass house. Glasshouse...

"I mean when we sat down the other day and I was talking to you about the business; I was saying this and that, but in reality, I don't sell my dick. It is just was something to do, what man do you know would not want to have sex with a women and do not have to wake up next to her the next day. On the other hand, have to listen to her screaming and hollering, begging for money. Porn was my freedom I did not want responsibility. However every new thing gets old, I am older now I want different things in life." Shit... Stones to a glass house. Glasshouse...

"What is your meaning of love? Thomas..."

"It's having, butterflies in your stomach, days, months, and years after you first met. It's that feeling you get when nothing else in the world matters. It's staying up at night, talking knowing you should be sleeping, because you have to get up in the morning. It's like spending hours getting dressed and you never make it out of the house. Love is picking your mate over your friends, because you want too and don't have too. It's not evil, it doesn't hurt and it's not caged in. It's not hidden, and it's beautiful. Love doesn't control and it can't be forced. It's pure, and it's innocent." No Thomas... Stones to a glass house. Glasshouse...

"I want you to give me the hammer, and I want you to let me break down those walls of yours, brick by brick... then I want you to let me take your hand and I want us to build our foundation brick by brick. All we need is trust, loyalty, honesty, and love. I am far from perfect, and I don't expect you to be. I am willing to give you that... but you have to be ready and not ready because I am ready..."

"Yeah I am living on an unstable rollercoaster." I said trying to laugh the situation off. Stones to a glass house. Glasshouse...

"Yeah that's how I got to the states. I left my family back home in Cape Town, South Africa... when my parents split up I hated the man my mother married after. So once I got of age, I moved back home to my father's rich lands. My father owns hotels on Mahe' Island in Seychelles, home of the world's most beautiful blue waters of the Indian Ocean. My mother disowned me when I tried to go back to Cape Town to visit her. She is upset with me because I left her with an abusive man. She didn't want to listen to me; when I told her, he wasn't any better, than the man she had her children by. Just like you, I rebelled. My natural father was a very rich man, no African man or woman needs to wear a fur coat, let alone own one. My father owned about fifty fur coats. He had diamonds, and stacks of gold bars.

My Father house is about forty-seven-hundred square feet I am talking huge! Marble floors, walls made out of ivory and fourteen karat-gold crowning. I grew up like the immigrants...my family's wealth in Mahe' isn't on an African level. You know its levels in social status; my father rebelled on his family. My grandfather is maybe the wealthiest black man in Africa; he owns oil plants, down in Niger. When my father told him, he wanted to go into the hotel business. My grandfather laughed, he said tourist copper is chicken change. He said it was nothing; my grandfather didn't like to hustle.

His hands were pretty for a man. He worked hard don't get me wrong, but he didn't do the labor. Whereas my father, held the bricks in his buildings in his own two hands. He built his empire of luxury hotels, on Mahe' island; one by one, in the smoldering heat, that brings summertime to the African people, and you can't forget the downpour of the rainfall; the tropical lands endure.

My father Passed away the early part of last year, and my grandfather passed away a few months after I arrived in the states. They left me everything; I was twenty-two sitting on a billion dollars in a bank account. That billion do not include business revenue from the oil plants.

When my father died, me being his first-born son, only born son I inherited 3.5billion dollars, and a multi- billion dollar hotel business. So I guess my grandfather had the chicken change. And you know my mother came looking for a hand out; I gave her ten million and a house in Victoria, Seychelles.

I took care of my three sisters too. Then I woke up one day and walked away from it all. I returned to the states; and got lost in the exotic heavens. I did not want the responsibility; I loved having sex with women, who just thought I was a regular person like them. All the women back home just wanted to get close to me because of my wealth. I didn't work for my wealth I wasn't in to flashing my means... it don't mean nothing to me..." damn I gave all the wrong men a chance; loves cures was lingering...

My grandfather laughed, he said tourist copper is chicken change. He said it was nothing; my grandfather didn't like to hustle. My grandfather laughed, he said tourist copper is chicken change. He said it was nothing; my grandfather didn't like to hustle. Damn I married a monster.

Chapter 19

The Eye of the Gun

"**Y**o, we just made it..." Brian, said as the two of us jumped into the car I was driving. Chancy jumped into his, he was right behind me.

"You good man? Thank you." I replied...

"It's all love, I don't believe Stilks would shift us like that man that shit was crazy. How the fuck did Chancy get Sal?"

"I don't know man, what happened? And where is Dee... damn..." I said whipping my face.

"I know you are not thinking about going back..."

"I was man, I can't leave her like that..."

"Wasn't you going to bag her after all this man..."

"I was, but that was before all of this..."

"What are you talking about?"

"She was telling me the truth… shorty had my back the entire time. Kaliyah was wearing Dee's daughter neckless around her neck when I saw her."

"That little girl didn't have a neckless on in the picture Gee…"

"I know what I am saying is true… I gave it to Dee to give to her on her birthday. We was talking one day and she mentioned Journey being heir to the throne. I had my jeweler make it for her; and I gave it to Dee, when she met me out in Cali."

"Damn, you sure?"

"Yeah nigga I'm sure… I had Harry Winston design Journey a one of a kind Sunflower diamond Neckless and the plate was Diamond studded. I spent mad chicken change on that, damn her mom said Dee was at the house. I know she was at the house because I dropped her off there… I didn't know Sal was in there… they said Sal was there…"

"Let it go Gee, it's too hot… I know you don't want to hear this but they got her the Sensations got her… I'm sorry man…"

"I know love and the street code don't mix… damn this is too much… B!"

"We are going to get over this… I got you and you know that goat got you… we are your boy's man…" just like that, it became a three-man team. This was it. This was the game. It was time that I let go of my hurts and human like feelings. Although accepting I lost Dee yet again was

something I rather have not done… I rocked out.
I rocked out in her honor.

Working on the last hour of the twenty-four, I
was thirty-three years old. A statistic in the black
male population. Not many black men live to see
twenty-five. I lost so many black brothers around
me to a 187. I took a few lives with a 187, with my
own hands. Thirty-three, with all the money I
made. With all the money, I managed to save. The
houses the cars, the girls the clothes. My position
in the streets. None of that shit mattered to me.
Thirty-three I just want to watch my sons growing
up. Both my sons I owe Makhi a lot. A statistic…
I had to shake my feelings…

"Okay this is it… Omar screwed everything
up. He got mad because I put you in his spot. He
linked up to the Choppers when he met Dee's
husband. Whatever contract business they had
together, was their business… Thomas is Dee
husband he is related to Jahgie Estelle wasn't
lying that is his sister. That bitch in the trunk
Estelle is also married to Thomas. Dee's marriage
is only legal in the States. Yall know she moved to
fucking Africa with that nigga. This is how Dee
was caught in the middle of things.

When we took that drop off the docks, Omar
brought in behind my back… that is that money
he said I had of his… Maine Street was
vengeance. That is why I wasn't going to sweat it.
I wasn't going to let ride either. That Jasper shit
through me off. I was playing Carlos close I had
to watch him. He would have fucked up
everything. Carlos was riding with Omar he
wanted me to kill him. He wanted to watch me kill

him. That Carlos shot up my house the other night. Fuck Melly warned me about him... find the girl, we break even... if the Sensations took Dee out... her daughter is Heir." It took me minute to put everything I knew out on the table without showing I was weak.

I had pulled to the side of the road, and Chancy pulled up on the side of me. As we sat in our cars laying out the plan, I held on to my crown. In the back of my mind, I knew I couldn't trust him nor Brian not as I could before. When Brian rolled behind the car with me during the shootout, when he reached into his pocket to get his extra clip, he dropped some work... yellow stone Heroin packages. Sensation packaging. The beef between Omar and me tag teaming each other left the streets starving. My nigga's traded on me. This was it... I didn't even show Brian or Chancy the photo of Dee's daughter. How did he know about the neckless?

"Okay, whoever that is still answering the number to the kidnapper, said meet him for the exchange by the old oil refinery, on the back road." I decided to text the number, just in case one of these niggas phone ringed. With Sal in the trunk, the last man standing was Thomas. I drove off into the last half-hour, with two of my million years of enemies taking me to meet the eye of the gun...

Chapter 20

The Death of a Dynasty

The old oil refinery was dark. There was nothing there but trash people dumped, as if it was a landfill. I was looking for a hiding spot, if I needed one. I saw a dumpster to the far left. It was surrounded by garbage. I wasn't familiar with this back road. I probably only been back there once or twice. Many years ago. The only source of light we had came from the headlights on the cars. When we pulled up, we parked parallel to each other. Both Sal and Estelle was stripped naked, and duct-taped for the trade. That was how Uptown did business.

Sal took part in the murder of Chauncey. That was the only reason why Chancy pistol-whipped him. The only reason why he didn't come back with Dee. He wasn't worrying about her... I wish I would have known or else I would have blazed off myself in that house. Damn I was the only one I could trust. Ouch, that shit hurt. However, I was a gangster and I did gangster shit. That wasn't Thomas pulling up...

"That's not Thomas..." I commented.

"I don't know... looks like we got company fellas..." Chancy replied...Damn it was Craig, Sal's old boss... Carlos man. He was the old man Estelle said was riding out with Jahgie. Thomas was younger than both Dee and me.

"To who do I owe this pleasure too? You are a hard person to get to... we didn't have to go this far... damn my men was right. You play harder than Carlos. I will give it to you; you earned King of the Streets. You do know that title is impossible to last forever. Considering how you got there anyway. Do you remember that day you, Melly, Chauncey and Omar and what's that big motherfucker name is again... oh Big Bruce... yeah yall shagged ole Carlos... well that was half of my money. Did you really think we was going to let that slide?"

"Thank you, I am glad you think I am doing a good job. I am speechless. Here I go thinking this was due to some new shit... and this is old business. Damn why now Craig, I mean why not then?" I questioned...

"Your army was too strong... I had to wait for your empire to fall. It's the code of the streets. You know the game..." Damn he pulled ah me on me. I waited for Carlos to fall before I took over the spot, damn... but I wasn't Carlos.

Part 5

Damn

Just when I thought nothing else could go wrong. I was still laying between that pissy mattress and the dumpster. Fighting rats away, that ran around me. I checked my gun. I was only missing two from the clip. I had and extra clip in my bra under my vest. I took a deep breath when I found it. I made sure this time I put it in my front pocket. I couldn't take the chances of my shit falling into my underwear again.

Three cars pulled up, I could not see who it was, and I just knew it did not look right. I knew it was not the police, because I saw when the drivers of two of the cars, opened their trunks and both of them pulled out people. It could not have been Greg. I was the only one that was put in the back of the trunk. When Chancy and Stilks took Scott, Dale and Carlos bodies out of the house they took the truck Carlos was driving, and dumped it.

Oh shit I thought to myself, another car pulled up. That one I could see clear. Thomas... damn I said a prayer to myself...

The Death of a Dynasty... continues

"So we finally get to meet... sorry I'm late... the kid was hungry, where is her mother?"

"Who are you?" I asked...

"Funny you don't know me?"

"Naw... I don't know you..."

"I am Thomas, I brought out the Choppers... and I brought out the Sensations. I merged them... I see why you routed Omar... He was supposed to be here too. To give you your options. Oh by the way I am the one who married your bitch..."

"Never heard of you... you mentioned my options, enlighten me..."

"Omar told me you can be a little cocky... you know me nigga... I thought for three years she was mine... seems like you fucked my bitch..."

"Skip the kitten litter shit... What the fuck are you talking about?"

"This came to my Fortress... I was going to let Dee, do what she wanted. I wasn't going to inconvenience her; until I realized the bitch stole my chicken change... do you know what that is... Greg right..."

"You spoke to me like you knew me so I am assuming you know my name purple... what do that have to do with me?"

"I want my chicken shit..."then he tossed me a piece of paper... Chancy picked it up and handed it me... damn that fucking bitch... did it again...I pulled Estelle making her stand in front of me.

"You love her too? Tell me my options..."

"You are done... we are taking the Streets..." Craig replied.

"Damn just like that... tell me do you love her?" I said pointing at Estelle as I pulled the potato sack from off her head... she was light skin I am thinking he thought it was Dee... his eyes lit up.

"Essie..." he shouted. Then as fast as I could pull my gun out... I shot her in head. I couldn't waste bullets. I was surprised to see both Chancy and Brian exchanging fire with the enemy. I dodged behind the cars, dragging Sal's body. I do not know who gun shot him. I used him for protection.

Part 6

Bad bitch

Thomas ran like a bitch. For the life of me, I thought it was all a dream. I blanked and within seconds, my husband was gun fighting with my heart. I could not see Greg. Nevertheless, I saw Thomas hiding. I decided to prove my loyalty.

I had to have his back the other day he told me "I know I wasn't there for you then, but I will be damn if you will die in my arms, or if I was going to die in your arms... I would never put that on you and never would I want that feeling on me." I believed him... and that is what I was thinking about...

I was too late, and I had lost sight of Thomas. Greg was down on the ground and Sal lifeless body was laying on top of him. I slid real quick on the same side as them. I glanced real quick. I could not look at him... damn Greg... where was my daughter I thought... Chancy was near the other car reloading his gun. Thomas ran up right behind him and shot him.

Damn Brain traded. He dabbed Thomas pound. I blanked. Then I looked up... Brian walked to the car I had seen Thomas pull up in, I don't think he saw me. Pop, Pop... I aimed and I shot him... damn... a strong force pulled me by my hair from behind.

"There you go darling..."

"Thomas get off me..." I yelled to a lot full of dead bodies...

Chapter 21

Torn

"**T**his was what you wanted? This isn't what you said. You know I believed you when you told me you love me. You said all of me and I could have all of you... is this the real you? Or is it the new you? I am confused... why? I never showed you this side of me because I meant every word I said. I guess you found out and this was your way of telling me. I know... baby I know. Here it is I thought you was taking trips to the states for work and shit... but naw love... you came to get your old love... I beat you at your own game.

See those niggas... wasn't your niggas... money don't solve problems when money wasn't what you used to know... you are nothing but a rich boy trying to live a hood nigga life. Tell me was it a fixed marriage or something real? Was it for the Choppers? You never loved me. See a nigga like you; make it hard for a woman like me to trust. You wined and dined me... you spoke that shit to me... you sweet-talked my panties off me. Was it all over some dusty pussy? Tell you the truth... I am over it. I should have never left Greg for you!

I put my all into you. I gave up everything I loved for you. I broke down my walls for you. I was all in. I told you I was taught by the best... the

Russians, bae. The streets raised me. I know a Chopper when I see one. You routed Omar, yet you blamed me. Well, it is over I cannot take it anymore. I am tired of you beating on me. I am tired of you cheating on me. You turned into everything you said you was not. You killed my sister! Its over... you killed Taylor. You never loved me! Instead, you used me... to get to Greg...

You set this bullshit up. Now you are mad because an American bad bitch fucked you over... rule number one of the Pete Dynasty... Pete's are Uptown... we always win. Give me my daughter back, and I will call this bull crap Chopper Sensations even... seven- eleven... that is how you play craps right?" I said crying out to Thomas, after I had managed to fight him off me. When his gun jammed, he ran behind the tree. I fired a shot to let him know my gun was loaded.

"In that trunk is your daughter, she is alive. However, It's C4 in the back seat. You shoot at me. I shoot the car. We all blow up. I love you Dee we can get over this. Journey is not mine Dee. I know Dee. Taylor had to die she was a rat. Damn we can get over this... you stole my money for Greg. I know Dee. We can get over that. Your pussy got dry when it came to me, yet it stayed ocean wet for that other nigga. I know Dee. The code of the streets right? That shit hurts you know..." Thomas was pleading for me to give in; but I knew he was going to trick me...

"Show me proof Journey is in the trunk, go get her I won't shoot." My baby was crying her heart out... "Thomas no...give her to me... Thomas.... Thomas............." I screamed

190

dropping my gun. Then as I dropped down on one knee... he pointed his gun to my baby's head... Pop. Pop. Pop. Pop. I closed my eyes then I exhaled. I was in shock... I was next...

Benediction

Heir to the Throne

I opened my eyes only to realize... Greg was a man of his word. Thomas... was dead. I looked over my shoulders, and standing over top of me, with blood all over him. Stood my King... Tears drowned my face. I was overjoyed with emotions. He was holding Journey in his arms. I picked Journey up and hugged her. She was screaming... as soon as she realized it was her Mommy holding her... she calmed down to quiet tears.

"I know I wasn't there for you then, but I will be damn if you will die in my arms, or if I was going to die in your arms... I would never put that on you and never would I want that feeling on me. I already lost you and that is hard to deal with."

"Thank you... I thought I lost you..." I hugged Greg tight...

"Naw, I wasn't leaving without you...We never got the chance to finish our conversation. Tell me the truth, as you know it; is Journey mine? That is what that paper said purple threw at me. You really was telling the truth. But what did you do with all of our money?"

"I told you, I wasn't lying... you been my day one...I did what Melly did... when she made me Heir to the throne."

"Can I hold her?" without hesitation... my King got to meet the Heir to his throne...and then on purpose...after we strapped Journey into the back seat next to me; Greg took the wheel of the car... I stopped him...

"Wait... we have to burn our tracks..." I said as I rolled down the window. I pulled Journey close to me and I held her open ear with my free hand...

"Dee we got to go..." Greg said as the both of us heard the police sirens coming from afar... I shot Thomas car up... I pulled and I pulled the trigger until the car exploded and flew up into the night sky...fire blow over the old oil tanker... all I know it was something like a movie... the fire spread swiftly! Greg then looked at me as I pulled my head back into the window he smiled.

"Ever hear of the boom-a-ring story. Shoot a boom-a-ring and if it comes back to you, it's yours to keep, and if it doesn't you lost it, then its finder keeper's looser weepers. Sitting in here, I am weeping, but I hope I am not a weeper... "

"I will always be your bad bitch..."

"No turning back... its me and you against the world... baby girl. I still got a connect in Mexico..."

"Greg... we have more than enough money...we can stop chasing Chicken Change... I got us...these streets don't love you like I do!" I replied...

"Damn girl, what am I going to do with you?"

"Promise me no matter what happens, we won't allow nothing to come between the King and his Queen."

"Loyalty, trust, honest... Dee, promise to never stop loving me... here you can have your crown back... inside every real bad bitch there is a Queen!"

"King I got you!" I replied...

"No, Queen we got each other..."

"True... we reloaded on them nigga's" I said laughing... as we traded places driving, we drove off to the point of no return... who would have ever thought I would end up on the run with my princess and MY KING!

Thank you for reading,

The Final Chapters

Of

Chicken Change:

The code of the Streets Tied up in a Love Affair.

LaToya Shahira Williams

The Visions

In

My Head

Productions

For information regarding permission, send an email to

LSW writers for The Visions in My Head productions

At

LSWwriters@yahoo.com

Keep in touch with LWS writers Follow us on Instagram: @thevisionsinmyhead

Catch us on Facebook: The Visions in My Head Productions

A note from the author

In every vision holds a story. The visions in my head I once kept to myself, because I once feared the opinions of others. Fear in hiding who you are will hold you back, from being the person you was born to be! Be who you are because there is no one like you. Dream big; turn all of your black and white dreams into color. Share your gifts and talents. There is no right or wrong answer. No is not a setback, behind every No... a Yes will follow! However, if you are scared you will never know!

-LaToya Shahira Williams

Readers...

Do you want to meet LSW Writer, LaToya Shahira Williams?

Simply write to LSW writers for The Visions in My Head Productions, and make your next book club event, even more special...

Email LSW Writers @LSWwriters@yahoo.com

Or

Catch our writers in a city, or event near you...

Chicken Change Reloaded

Authored by LaToya Shahira Williams

The Visions in my Head Productions

ISBN-13: 978-0692400661

ISBN-10: 0692400664

BISAC: Fiction / Urban

It was once a Vision in my Head!